This book is a dedication to

all the beautiful people

who worked or walked inside

Granny Bubbles Sweet Shop

Acknowledgements

My amazing Mum,

my beloved husband and my kids

Thank you for the encouragement

The Author

So, here I am! My very first book. I never in my wildest dreams thought I could write so much as an A4 page, let alone an entire book. Mr Durant, my English teacher, would fall off his Spanish retirement sun lounger at the thought of me writing anything at all! The only evidence of *MY* writing skills as far as he was concerned were displayed solely in the punishment lines, he sent me during detention each week. I was far too easily distracted and busy messing around in class to be interested in English.
I sat next to Joanna Raymond in Mr Durant's class. Collectively our English knowledge stretched to reading the ingredients on the back of Joanna's Tangy Toms Tomato Puff crisp packet, which were hidden behind her 'Animal Farm' book by George Orwell. We spent many an hour avoiding tedious classwork, giggling and writing - mostly on each other's arms as opposed to in our textbooks. I loved his class, but not for the right reasons. So, nobody will be more surprised about this book than Mr Durant!

L A Knighton x

Invisible Introduction.

Now, I know for a fact that some people *NEVER* read introductions. I know this because I am one of them. I don't think I have ever read a single book introduction in my entire life. If there is a shortcut to pleasure, I will take it every time.

So, suppose you *are* a sensible person who savours every one of life's experiences, including book introductions. In which case, quite frankly, you should be knighted by the Queen for services to literature. This introduction is indeed for YOU dear reader.

To prove my *'introduction-avoidance'* theory, I will leave a little joke between us, with the answer at the end of the book and don't you dare skip to the last page. It will be a test to see if you have read this text.

I have chips for tea blah blah blaaaaaaaah—filling space. Blaah blaaah blab la blah. With fresh bread and creamy butter. Salt and pepper and an egg to dip the chips in. Blah blaaaaaaaaaah. Not a soul is reading this anyway. But just in case you *are* reading this, I suppose I could tell you a little something about this book.

It is true that Granny Bubbles Sweet Shop was a real-life sweet shop. For quite some time actually!

There are over 5400 High Streets in Britain. My High Street was located in one, right in the middle of England, in the heart of beautiful Northamptonshire. Some might say it is the Earth's epicentre.

My shop was situated in a Victorian shoemaking town called "Rushden". It was a great place to have a shop. Right up until a colossal, shiny new, out of town shopping arcade opened and sent us to the high-street-shop-heaven with all the other butchers, bakers and candlestick makers.

The sweet shop was named in honour of my very own Granny, who was called 'Bubbles' in her childhood. Later, when she was my Granny, she became "Granny Bubbles". Poor old Granny Bubbles passed away before I opened the sweet shop. The shop was an ode to her name, and I think you will agree it was a magnificent name too. So magnificent it deserved a fabulous book to be written in her honour. Taaa Daaa!!! Here it is...

This story is very lightly inspired by the fantastic, loyal, talented customers we served in Granny Bubbles Sweet Shop. We had an incredible array of custom. Like the Dolly Mixtures addict Doris, who once brought her 1950's wedding knickers in to show me, and little Kelly, who came banging on the door for sweets at 9 o'clock on a Saturday morning because her pet gerbil had eaten its brother. Only fizzy cola bottles would make her feel better.

In the book ahead (after this pretend introduction), you will meet the young Violet Rose. A happy girl that stands up for herself and others. Her self-confidence grows in strength after dealing with many unkind and mean people. From venomous girls to thick-headed boys who bully people at school, not forgetting her meat-headed twin brothers, that tried to make her life a misery on the farm where she grows up. Each situation makes her stronger and arms her with all the tools needed for later life. Before long, she takes zero stick off anybody. Vile Mr Wallops, the physics teacher, gets his comeuppance and is taught a lesson by Violet Rose and her best friend Clarabell.

As Violet Rose (Bubbles) morphs into a woman, she marries and has plenty of children. Eventually, she finds herself in a position of independence and decides to put her dreams into action. With her last savings, she follows her lifelong dream of opening her very own sweet shop.

From ponies to pythons, barristers to bonbons. If you want Gobstopping Gossip from a busy sweet shop, then look no further. Enjoy tales of pirates, Parma Violets and stories of spies, sweets and sherbet.

So, grab a bag of your favourite bonbons or sherbet lemons. (You will probably have to buy supermarket sweets or buy online unless you are lucky enough still to have an independent sweet shop in your town?) If not, I can recommend 'The best you ever had Cola Cubes' from www.aquarterof.co.uk. They are immense!

Sit back and immerse yourself in a few hours of fluff and fiction. Blah Blah Blah Jelly Bears and Humbugs. Brush your teeth after you eat sweets. But you probably won't, like you are probably not reading this introduction now. Thank you for not reading. Onwards dear reader. Onwards. I have got to go I have an itchy bum.

L A Knighton x

"What do you call a lamb covered in chocolate?"

Contents

Chapter One

Godzilla and the Pony

I HATE the cold. But I would rather freeze my digits off than be near that fat-headed old cabbage. I had been polishing a box of seventy-four, freshly delivered, Braeburn apples for the last twenty minutes in the biting cold. I was so thorough that their shiny little red and green skins glistened in the low autumn sun. If these did not sell by the end of the day, I would kiss old onion bunion on the bald head in defeat. I was THAT confident in my workmanship. Of course, the granny smiths, pink ladies and gala apples required a buff up too. Still encased in their wooden display crates looking less than inviting. I absolutely didn't mind being outside the front of the grocers, freezing one bit if it meant I was further away from the carrot cretin. There were boundless vegetable related names I called him in my head and under my breath. A more deluded old broccoli brain you have never met. He was deplorable.

I looked down at my watch and grinned to myself. 'FANTASTIC!!!!' I thought. A sneaky wide grin beamed across my face. The millisecond I looked down at my wristwatch, I could hear his giant, hairy fist clenched and banging on the window from inside the grocers. "Get on wiy it Gurl!!!! Never mind what time it is. Tain't time for you to be looking at thy watch, that's for certain. Them there Gala apples will not polish thyselves. I am not paying you to gorp at your watch all day Gurrrrl." So yelled the gruff voice from inside the Grocers.

That was Mr Plum. My Yorkshire boss, who I deemed as mad as a box of kumquat. He was terribly unhealthy in appearance for a man who sold vegetables for a living. He constantly suffered from crusty gout in his toes. Amongst other ailments, he was partially deaf in one ear, so he shouted every waking moment, mostly at me. Mr Plum came from a long line of grocers. His father was a grocer, his father's father was a grocer, and his uncle was a grocer too. He took every opportunity to tell anyone who would listen about his lineage.

Unfortunately for me, he came to Rushden in the 1960s. He married his long-suffering wife. She kept well away from the grocery shop. She probably revelled in the quiet; I was not so lucky.

Mr Plum was very aptly named for his profession. He was enormous and bald with a big fat belly that looked like he ate more pie than vegetables. "Plum's me name, and plums are me game, " he bellowed in his booming deep Yorkshire accent. If you were fortunate enough not to see him, you would most certainly hear him coming.

"Yes Mr Plum. I'm hard at it Sir." I mouthed sweetly through the glass window. Then followed a further fist bang on the window. "And bring them King Edwards t'front and move em t'where Maris Pipers are t' left. Folk can't see em properly there. What's the use in me buying em if folk caaant see em? Makes no sense. Get on wiy it Gurl." He roared, without taking a breath, parking his gigantic body behind the counter on a very forgiving tall stool. Turning his back on me to his piping hot cup of tea in his toasty warm shop. "Yes Mr Plum. I'll get to it right now." I mouthed, painting on a false toothy smile. As he turned to his newspaper and continued the daily crossword.

Out of his view for lipreading, I became a little brave. "I'll do it all then, shall I? God forbid an overgrown Brussel bonce like you move your own King Edwards" That wretched old boot has never done a full day's work in his life. "I'll polish the apples, sweep the pavement, place the signs out, you just stay in the warm and drink tea whilst you watch me, you lazy, soul-crushing, crusty old earwig." He looked up for a moment, and I repeated my best toothy smile before he snarled and slurped a huge gulp from the mug of tea that he had made only for himself.

The beetroot cheeked pleb didn't give me a minute the moment I stepped foot in that grocery shop. From the start of my working day until I clocked off at the end. If I heard "Get on wiy it gurl" once, I heard it a thousand times in a day.

It was just a temporary job and not my life choice. My real passion was writing. I studied English literature during term time, and when I came home, I laboured in the beetroot boot camp for free fruit and cash. It made his tyrannic behaviour more bearable, knowing that one day I would never have to listen to his bombasts EVER again.

I moved all of the 20kg bags of Maris Pipers as well as six bags of 25kg King Edwards to Mr Plums precise military coordinated grid referenced location, I took a fresh clean cloth from my apron and set to work polishing the pink lady apples.

"Mek sure those Danver carrots are nice and uniform in those boxes and fluff up those green carrot tops will yer and while you're there, give em a water spray to hydrate em. No point in my buying them if folk can't see how wonderful they are."

Mr Plum took his fruit and veg VERY seriously and he could delegate with gusto. But as long as I was outside the front of the shop, I was happy. Far away from his military briefings of button mushrooms and the price of The Prince of Wales's organic raspberries.

I sneaked a look at my watch again, 9:46 am and there they were... bang on time. It brightened up my mornings no end to schnozzle on other folks' business while they meandered into the town to complete their daily chores.

Finishing the pink lady's apples and now onto the gala apples I slowed the pace down. I didn't want to go back into the shop too soon.

Closer and closer to the green grocers, the chatter gained a little more volume until I could finally hear them clearly. I leaned in a little towards their direction.

"D'you know Margo; the sun is so bright today; it highlights all of the grey bristly hairs on your chin... ohhhh look, and your top lip. They glisten ever so brightly in this low light. You look like one of those old Turkish barbers. I bet you can see them hairy corkers from Constantinople!" Grinned Margery rudely.

Margo raised her hand to her chin and slowly felt the short prickles. She was sure she was on top of her personal care but, clearly not, according to mean old Margery. Quick as a flash, she halted in her steps and looked Margery dead in the eye and snipped back.

"I'm glad you feel so comfortable in pointing out a personal maintenance issue Margery. Maybe it is OK for me to point out one of yours? I can get rid of my chin hair Margery, but there is absolutely nothing you can do with your crumply ancient old cabbage face. I can't decide if your face reminds me of a wrinkly walnut or a bag of broken biscuits, and not even the tasty custard creams, more like a cruddy old bourbon. I feel quite sorry for you. If I had your wrinkles, I'd be straight off to the doctors for a facelift. Mind you, you'd need a crane winch to lift your eye bags because they are sooooo saggy." She replied calmly with a sting, side smiling to herself at her quick wit and rapid response.

Each day, three sisters, Margo, Margaret and Margery, strolled into the town's High Street to buy their bread, meat and vegetables for the day ahead. They walked at the same pace, all in a neat line down thankfully stopping at the grocers each day. They very slowly tottered to the grocers, bakers and butchers without fail every weekday morning. Which was fantastic for me because I could not get enough of them.

They lived all in a splendid grand Victorian house. The same place that they had all grown up in together, which fortunately stood within walking distance of the town centre. They were, you see, very elderly identical triplets. When I say 'identical', there was really no way of telling them apart. Only they knew who they were! Each triplet was a carbon copy of the next. This made the personal insults even more hilarious.

They had freckles in the same place, hairlines that curled in the same direction, and even their ears were slightly uneven, with one ear distinctly higher than the other. It was a little like looking in a circus three-way mirror. The ladies all dressed identically just to make it even more tricky to tell them apart.

Each triplet wore a uniform of archetypal English granny-issue clothing, circa 1945 and all three were furnished with immaculate beige Mackintoshes coats with matching material belts around the belly. Under the Mackintosh peeped three A-line dense brown woollen skirts with a petticoat waving out daringly from under the hem. For all I knew, there could have been feathers, fur or fish scales underneath them macs. They were seldom seen wearing anything else regardless of the weather. They each sported American tan tights and comfy grey nanna shoes that I have never seen sold anywhere in the world, but all nannas of a certain era seem to have them. The triplets had grey-blonde hair. Each in rollers. Each with a cream chiffon scarf, neatly hugging the curlers into place and each pulled along a different coloured red, blue or yellow tartan shopping trolley behind them. The trollies were the only way of telling them apart. They were quite a sight.

On the grapevine it was said that unfortunately for them, they had never had the opportunity to be real-life nannas, for none of them had ever been married at all. They had no children to call their own. At no time had they convinced three separate gentlemen to be daring enough to take them all on at once. In the early days, any boyfriends that came along were soon sent packing. The bickering was too intense, and not many boys fancied being in the firing line. They came as a package and were a force to be reckoned with. No man was brave enough. So, they had made a long life together and were happy, wealthy and inseparable.

They were drawing closer. This was peak volume time, and I was excited.

"ACTUALLY...", waded in Margaret the third sister, stopping her yellow tartan shopping trolly in its tracks and sticking her two penneth in. Purely for the joy of stirring the sisters' torment up a little further.

"I have always thought you are both rather ordinary and if you don't mind me saying also quite grey. I often thank my lucky stars that I don't look anything like either of you. Also, I am far more intellectual, attractive and amusing than both of you put together, I always have been. I always will be. It's a shame for you both really. I could have been a movie star if you two ugly moose heads hadn't ruined my chances!"

Margo and Margery screwed up their faces in utter doubt like petulant six-year-olds. Then doubled over laughing at their sister's delusion, each leaning on their own tartan shopping trollies for support. Margo laughed so hard; she crossed her legs as if to prevent a wee escaping.

Once Margo had caught her breath, she panted her reply. "Hells, bells, buckets and spells girl. You have a face for radio Margaret, not for Hollywood. Your face is the worst face out of all of ours. You could make the wicked witch of the west's wart look pretty if you stood next to it. You're only short of a broom yourself. If I were you, I would want to be careful a house doesn't fall on me." quipped Margo, still catching her breath from laughing so hard. Margery nodded in agreement with everything Margo was saying.

Once they had gathered themselves together, they continued. Rattling their shopping trollies along the bumpy cobbled pavement, they slowly edged towards Mr Plum's Green Grocers, still within earshot.

"Shut up Margo, you old carcass. I was only thinking this morning, when you stepped out of the bathroom, that you reminded me of a swollen rhino in a dressing gown. It quite put me off my porridge." Margaret laughed.

"You outrageous old turnip. I do not look like a swollen rhino. I bet it was like looking in the mirror when you looked into your porridge bowl this morning." Sniggered Margo. Most amused with her own response.

To the untrained eye, from a distance, they looked like gentle, 4ft tall, old ladies who wouldn't say "Boo!" to a goose. In confectionery terms, they were comparable to fluffy marshmallow with an arsenic centre. I am sure they did love each other dearly and couldn't live without one another really. But they seemed to be comfortably quite ruthless, at times brutal and nearly always awful to each other. In a way in which only triplets who had spent every waking moment together could be.

Here they were, right in front of me. I gently enquired. “Good morning, Miss Frost, Miss Frost and Miss Frost. What can I get you today?” Now, I have heard the way that they communicate with each other time and time again. Brutal, sharp, sarcastic and snippy. But when they spoke to outsiders their tone was sweet, soft, articulate and gentle.

“Three Danvers carrots, one head of broccoli and three baked potatoes please” replied all three in harmony at once. It took a bit of getting used to hearing them all reply at once, but I was used to it now. I hurried to collate the order. The sooner they were on their way again, the quicker they returned to being the REAL Frostettes and the more it made me chuckle.

I observed that if they ever stopped to chat to anyone else outside their trio, they snapped clean out of their foul dialogue and were all as pleasant as could be to the recipient. Each would stick to a sensible, friendly conversation about the weather or the price of fish. It was only my well-trained ear that could hear what the triplets were really like. They gave me endless mornings of amusement. Watching them flit between venom and sweetness was a joy. Elderly ladies are phenomenally good at quality sibling abuse. They have years of practice you see.

I wrapped the carrots, broccoli and baked potatoes in a brown paper and popped one of each item in each of their trollies. That way nobody would be pulling any more than the next.

As they shuffled away from Mr Plums' Green Grocers, I could still just snatch the end of their carnage conversation. "Well, Bernard Tuffet was as bald as that parsnip anyway. He ran clean away from your mooted face so fast his corduroy trousers nearly set on fire. You couldn't keep a man if ...." and the insults tailed off from earshot until the same time tomorrow. I couldn't wait.

At least I could see the next regulars coming my way, and it filled me with further delight. It didn't seem to fill my bossy Mr Plum with much pleasure. He apparently wanted some work done. How dull! I pretended to move some broccoli around the box to look busy for the sake of being paid, but it wasn't long before my next distraction swanned by.

First came the dishevelled blond lady, wearing muddy green wellies with a bright fuchsia pink fur coat. Not for the first time either. She was, as usual, moving at a trot and was guiding a small dappled grey pony on a short rope. I should have been more alarmed, and I was, during my first week of work at the grocers, but now I was used to them.

The pony had an odd name 'John!'. Which always made me smile. Who would call a pony 'John'? To my mind he should have been called Rainbow or Munchkin? Or something equally soft and mushy. But, no, 'John' was how people greeted him just as they would a human. "Morning, John!" Folks would say as if meeting up with a golf buddy or the local tyre fitter. After a pat and a stroke, they would bid him a good day. "Have a great day, John!" They would say as if he would reply, "I will do, Steve, you look after yourself". It was most peculiar given the time to think about it.

He was a good-natured beast, small as you like but with the confidence of a racehorse stud. He was a chipper chap too, and why wouldn't he be? With his exceptional popularity and excellent social standing, he was utterly spoilt. Occasionally he crossed the road onto our side and if he was allowed a carrot, I gave him one from the past-it pile. (Making sure the big fat potato face wasn't watching or he would charge me for the carrot).

There were no paddocks to be seen for a good few miles. We were right in the middle of a busy town, and I often wondered how far and where exactly they had both originated from. I meant to ask, but I always forgot. I had pondered if they had walked either many miles to get here from a farm out of town or maybe, I daydreamed, perhaps they lived in a two-up two-down terrace house close to town? Avoiding any potential work, I began to contemplate; I imagined the two of them in the house together of an evening settling down by the coal fire. Each with a hot cup of cocoa with cream and marshmallows. Welly lady on a comfy armchair and John the pony casually perched on a tuffet in the living room. Both watching a gritty police soap opera or similar. It was a cosy scene which I am sure only existed in my head because the reality of a pony in your living room would be, well, smelly?

"Av you seen to them Jaffa oranges yet gurrrl? Them stickers all want to be pointing the same way. Mek'em look tidy gurl, I SAY... MEK'EM LOOK TIDY!!!!" Boomed Mr Plum snapping me out of my daydream.

The thought of the marshmallows was starting to make me feel hungry. Off they casually trotted past Freeman, Hardy and Willis shoe shop, the drapers and then further down the street. They stopped for chats and pats all the way. From children in push buggies to pub landlords putting their pavement signs out leaning in for a fuss. Everyone knew John. Whilst his fellow equestrian family may have been staring blankly at a soggy tree in the middle of a chilly paddock, John had things to do and people to see. Because you know, he was on his way to the sweet shop for his daily dose of herbal candy.

Each day, Welly Lady entered the sweet shop. John didn't, of course. There was a small hook outside, especially for him to be tethered to. I think there may have been a 'No Ponies' policy inside the shop, but I didn't see a sign.

Welly Lady ordered John two small squares of the Horehound flavoured fudge delicacies. I know this because I more than once have been behind her in the queue in the sweet shop. They looked a bit like crumbly fudge squares but tasted like cough medicine. Indeed, not my idea of fun, but pardon the pun... it's horses for courses! It was his daily treat from his owner, and I'm sure it had nothing to do with the fact she had a mild addiction to flying saucers AND the need to exercise the wee fellow at the same time. She was clearly killing two birds with one stone. Which I thought was genius. Flying saucers are so addictive after all, and if you are going to have a vice, then this one is the one to have. They enjoyed their treats and carried on with their trot through town.

All manner of beings used the high street. If the sun was shining and warm in the summer, the Pet Shop Man would walk his pets down the High Street too. It would not be uncommon to see a black and white skunk called “Buddy”, who liked nothing better than to do handstands along the High Street, stopping to sniff lamp posts and eat the occasional path dandelion.

"Sorry about that!" Pet shop man would mention if anybody was accidentally sprayed with

Buddy Skunk juice. Buddy wasn't very good at spraying as he didn't seem to hold much in his little spray tank. But just sometimes, if he didn't like the look of you, he could try, and it might just catch your shoes. Buddy wasn't very keen on the parking warden. In fact, some days, it seemed he saved all his smelly but small pong juice up just for the poor man.

Pet shop man also brought his Gold Pygmy Goat called Hopper. Hopper would be found scampering along on a long rope. Stopping to help himself to the bay tree leaves outside the gift shop or drop poo pellets on the pavement. The town council sweeper was only too happy to sweep up the poo and pop them in the street flower baskets. It was apparently the best fertilizer and produced magnificent award-winning blooms. Hopper was a helpful ecosystem all of his own.

Another regular wandering by was 'Godzilla' the giant monitor lizard, out for a stroll if it was hot and warming his belly up on the hot pavement. He was now 9 years old and fully grown, weighed 70 kg and was 2.5 meters long. He was huge. They can live up to 30 years you know! Godzilla had been confiscated from some horrid animal smuggler's hand luggage at the airport. He was a long way from his Indonesian home. As a juvenile back then, Godzilla was only 26cm long and had been found by customs officers stuffed in a Leicester City football sock. He was rehomed with Pet Shop Man because of his expertise as a reptile specialist.

Godzilla had a bright red body harness and a long extender lead. He would casually and very slowly meander along the pavement, puffing up his chest as if he owned the place, thumping past the hairdressers and health food shop. I had seen it with my own eyes so often that it became entirely normal. Pet shop man would warn open-mouthed shocked people to stand aside. You can imagine what people thought when they had just popped into the High Street for a spot of banking to seen Godzilla for the first time wandering along the High Street. "Don't worry, Godzilla doesn't have any teeth anymore. He can't harm you."

His teeth fell out one by one when he first arrived in England. Nobody knew why. Probably the trauma. Very sad indeed, he had to have his food mushed up too.

Folks didn't seem as willing to stop and chat when Godzilla was on his travels like they did with John. He tended to clear a path all the way. I'm not sure John and Godzilla ever crossed paths. Come to think of it, I'm not sure a Shetland pony has EVER crossed paths with a Monitor Lizard?

It was a wonderful High Street that surprised me every day with the colourful lives of all that use it. I could think of no better place to people watch alongside avoiding the giant Yorkshire pudding.

Chapter Two

Cola Pips and Chocolate Pots

Mr Plum had been unbearable that morning. “Line up them there conference plums gurrl, NOOOOOOOOOOO NOT THAT WAY gurrl. THAT WAY. For the love of pie gurl, divant yu ever listen.” He boomed at me like I was a toddler. “That beetroot wants seeing to an all. They look deranged” He barked.

“Yes Mr Plum. It is on my list” I sarcastically smiled. Although I don’t really know why I smiled because the act of smiling was wasted on the podgy fingered old ogre.

"LIST!!! What list? I will believe that when I see it." Bellowed Mr Plum. "I can't abide addled folk. And you gurl are addled. List my eye! University eckers like I'll go t'foot of t' stairs if you mek owt of your sen. Blether! That's all it is. I say BLETHER!!!! is what you are gurl. I'm the gaffer around here and I'll do the lists and you can think on if you are going to spend the time, I have given you shekel's for, gawping at t' lady cows out that window. Those courgettes won't get themselves in line gurl, I say GET THEM IN LINE gurl."

Roughly translated

"LIST!! I will believe that when I see it. I can't stand lazy people; I will be ever so surprised if you make anything of yourself. You are talking nonsense. Nonsense I say! I am the boss here and I pay you to work and not to look

out of the window at the lady birds. Kindly line the courgettes up"

Mr Plum was exhausting. It wasn't even Frostette o'clock yet and his voice was comparable to fingernails running down a blackboard in my ears. The Frostettes came and went. Each with onions and red potatoes for their liver and onion dinner and baking apples for a crumble. Today's chosen mockery topic was who had the worst nasal hair (Margery apparently) and which triplet could make the best crumble. (Margo claimed this crown but Margaret trumped her with her frozen butter recipe, which I discovered makes a crumble extra crunchy).

John had been by for his horehound candy and Hopper had stopped by Mr Plums for the carrot tops I had saved him. Mr Plum was adamant I charge for them. Mr Plum boomed “Charity begins at um; I’ve rent to pay and feeding goats for free is not part of my five-year business plan. I won’t retire on giving away my wares for FREE!!! That’ll be tenpunce please” His words left me speechless and ten pence lighter. Hopper had more heart than him and as parting gift dropped recycled carrot tops by his King Edwards. Mr Plum’s head turned a raging plum tint picking up the brown nuggets.

It was now lunchtime, and before I imploded inside my mind, my ears ringing from Mr Plums rants it was time to get out. Back out into the cold fresh air and bright blue autumn sky and to treat my lugholes to some peace and to a change of scenery. Thinking about John the pony and his love of Horehound Candy had highlighted the sweet shop in my mind, and I found myself daydreaming of Cola Pips. Suddenly, Cola Pips were all I could think of, and I had worked myself up into such a frenzy, I could practically taste them. I could feel my ears tickling, my jaw aching and I was salivating just at the thought of popping those tangy pips in my mouth.

After completing the size sorting of Amalfi Lemons, I grabbed a £1 coin from my purse, my bobble hat "Just going on my lunch Mr Plum." I yelled out to the back room where he was busy making himself a 'Brew of the finest Yorkshire tea for ONLY Yorkshire folk'

"Don't you dally back gurl, those Persian limes need displaying and the Blood oranges need moving forward of the Jaffa's to get sold quicker………" and on he rattled but I closed the door behind me Muting his din. It was my time now.

The crisp cold air slapped my cheeks and refreshed my skin of his gloom. I made my way quickly down the High Street and headed to not just John's happy place, but my own too.

I found myself picking up speed the closer I got to the sweet shop, dreading that it might be closed. Which was very unlikely, but I had talked myself into a bit of a panic. It was as if my life depended on being able to buy a bag of my all-time favourite sweets. The closer I got, the more I panicked. What if the sweet shop had been closed or worse still, was out of stock? I crossed the threshold of the shop like the front runner in a Pamplona bull chase, pushing the door with such force, the vintage brass bell attached to the back of the door made a violent ringing noise. The lady behind the glass counter looked up at me a bit shocked and slightly bemused but welcomed me in with a smile anyway.

"Good morning!" she chirped with one eyebrow raised. "In a bit of a hurry?"

I bashfully replied that I was "Starving" and apologised about my bullish entry. I stopped and took a deep breath, got myself together and meandered in, slowing right down in awe.

Right behind me the door crashed open causing the brass shop bell to jiggle like crazy once again. In wandered a small blonde boy with a worried look on his face.

"Edward!!! Whatever is the matter?" enquired the lady behind the counter. I turned around. I could see his mother was outside the window, deep in chatter to a fellow mother, each with a pram filled with pink frilly toddlers. Their toddlers touching toe to toe. Whatever or whoever they were talking about had clearly led them into a deep gossip coma because they hadn't even noticed Edward was absent and that he had gone into the shop alone.

Edward stood frozen with tears blurring up in his eyes. "Mrs Bubble Lady, I need some 'elp" He stepped forward and tilted his back to show two shiny foil covered chocolate footballs wedged up his left nostril and again on his right. "Good lord, Edward! How did those get up there?"

"I thought I could save them for later so that I didn't have to share them with my little sister. She always takes my sweets so I hid them, but it's making it hard for me to breathe when I close my mouth and I think Mummy might be a bit mad that I did it too. Will YOU get them out please Mrs Bubble Lady?" A tiny tear rolling down his flushed face. Snorting slightly, forgetting he had wedged chocolate in his air holes.

"Oh, right. I see." She pondered calmly, and there was a long silence from all of us. "Right, I've got it. Close your mouth and hold your breath Edward, now push all of that air up to your nose and see if you can shoot them out with the pressure of your breath?" I got the feeling this was not her first rodeo in this situation.

Edward took a deep breath in and turned his whole head pink with sheer determination not to be caught by his mother. With an almighty blow and a splurt, the left nostril released a red and white foil football which rolled across the shop floor at speed, accompanied by an unsightly fountain of snot.

"Right, put your finger on the empty nostril and do the same again and blow with all of your might."

Out shot a black and white foil chocolate football.

"Well done Edward. I don't think you should use your nostril as a hiding place anymore. You might need to think of another plan?" said the lady with a smirk.

Edward nodded frantically in agreement. The shop owner handed him a fresh stripy bag to put the balls in. “Right Edward, take them home and put them in the bin.”

“Thank you, Mrs Bubble Lady.” He wiped his snotty nose on his jumper sleeve, turned on his heels and headed to the door, looking VERY pleased he could breathe through his nose again but even more pleased his mother had not seen his situation unfold. He trundled outside and handed the bogey covered footballs in the bag straight to his little sister in the pram. His mother gave him a pat on the head for being so kind and off they went with the mother not knowing a thing. The shop lady smirked, shook her head and winked at me. I stared, bewildered at what had just happened and in awe of her patience and kindness. I, unhelpfully, had stood as still as possible throughout the whole debacle. Hoping not to get covered in snot.

Eventually, I shook myself out of my daze, and looked around. Even though I had visited the sweet shop so many times before, I was always blown away at the sheer volume of choice.

The selection seemed to grow larger and larger every week. There was jar upon jar, row after row of colours, smells and confectionery bliss. Sweet peanuts, bonfire toffee, banana toffee, Chocklick, cinder toffee. It seemed endless.

As I reached halfway through the shop, stepping up my pace, making sure my cola pips were there. There they were a full jar nestled in between the sherbet pips and fruit pips. They were absolutely what I wanted.

Wide-eyed as I continued to survey, I asked: "Please could I have one pound's worth of Cola Pips?" I picked up the heavy jar and handed it to her.

"A pound in money or a pound in weight?" I stopped and pondered for a moment. Could I genuinely munch through one pound in weight of cola pips??? The answer was a resounding 'Yes, most certainly', but unless I wanted to fall into a diabetic coma when I returned to Mr Plums, I had better be sensible. " I'll just take a quid's worth if that's ok?"

The lady chuckled and popped my heavenly spheres of sweet delight into a small red and white stripy paper bag. She flipped the bag over and twisted it around the top to close it. She held out her open hand awaiting payment in one hand, whilst holding the cola pips to ransom in the other. I passed over my shiny one and only new one-pound coin whereby she released the imprisoned pips to me with a smile. I delved straight into the bag as quickly as I could, barely giving her time to put her money in the till. The pips were small but mighty, smothered in a tiny coat of miniature spikey sugar crystals that were rough on your tongue. Once you had sucked away the crystal sugar coating then followed a sharp, smooth slap of cola flavour that whooshed around inside your mouth, sparking a taste sensation.

Now, I am not the kind of girl who can take one pip and pop it in my chops and get on with my day. I ram them in my face like a filthy bandit is standing over my shoulder, ready to snatch them away from me. No way Jose! Thoughts flickered through my mind, such as 'What if I were to die before I'd finished the bag?' That wouldn't do at all.

I very slowly advanced towards the door, still perusing what else I needed in my life or maybe I could buy next time when I had more money with me. Maybe some milk teeth, coconut ice or Edinburgh rock? My eyes open wide and greedy. I was sucking in as much as my senses could fit in. I had only just at that moment wondered how such these little delights had made their way into my life at all. I had been eating them since I was a little girl, but it had never occurred to me to consider where they had mysteriously come from. They just appear in my possession like magic, and all I ever had to do was pay with money!

I turned on my heels and made eye contact with the lovely lady, who was still cleaning out her weighing pan for the next customer.

Suddenly I found myself engaging, quite unexpectedly. "Where do these Cola Pips come from?" I half-whispered with a mouthful of far too many pips still sloshing around inside.

She wiggled her fingers and waved her latex-gloved hands in front of herself. Rather bashfully, she replied "I make them Dear, with my own fair hands. Well actually I have a machine in the workshop to help me, but I boil all the ingredients myself and the machine shapes them."

She pointed with her thumbs to an open door right behind her. I was quite taken aback by the fact that she made these herself. Like all things in the modern-day, I had just assumed they were mass manufactured and had been bought in from a giant wholesaler from some far-flung country. “I handmake most of the sweets in the shop myself.” she informed me.

I gazed around at what seemed like a gazillion jars on the shop shelves, all twinkling in the reflection of the shop lighting and concluded this was one busy lady indeed. With my mind running into overdrive, possibly due to the sugar fix, I wondered what her workshop kitchen must be like to produce all this brilliance.

"How amazing!" I squeaked with a slurping of pips and grossly nearly letting a few escape. "Can I see where you make them?" I enquired rather cheekily. Not for a moment thinking the lady would oblige.

She smiled and replied, "Of course, come around here Dear and I can show you where the magic happens".

I was aware I am brutally nosey, but she appeared to be quite delighted that someone had taken any notice of her business at all. Quite happily, she escorted me behind the counter and through a door towards the back of the shop and behind a colourful door curtain, made of rainbow dyed ribbons reaching to the floor. They parted and opened into the most fantastic confectionery kitchen right in front of my eyes. It had been there all this time, and I had never given it a thought. It felt like I had entered a top-secret world. I felt my heart race a little faster. I had never seen anything like it. To describe it to you, it was probably the size of an average living room, covered in white tiles on the floor, ceiling and walls. It was super clean and as fresh as you would want any food to be prepared in.

Neatly displayed glass jars perched on a purpose-built shelf. The eye level shelf wound around the room like a halo with all the elements that you would ever need for making every sweet in the land. Hundreds of them. Jars with pure oils of clove, aniseed, peppermint, lemon oil and orange oil. Flavours like cola, horehound, saspirella, liquorice and cherry. On another wall sat powdered colours, liquid colours and gel colours all snuggled next to each other like a rainbow of food colouring each in strict colour order. The jars were remarkably pretty, each with perfectly aligned labels and a shiny gold twisty lid.

Above a large gas cooking ring hung giant hooks imbedded in the white-tiled wall. On them hung a fabulous selection of polished giant Victorian copper boiling pans as big as the drum of a washing machine. The pans had two large iron handles that had been riveted solid on each side of the pan. I wondered how a little lady like her could pick those up, especially if they were full of toffee?

In the corner lay a large stockpile, reaching halfway up to the ceiling of huge brown paper sacks with 'English Sugar 25kg' stamped on them. Piled high behind the door were gigantic bright blue tubs, big enough to pop a toddler inside, each topped with a colourful yellow lid. Written on the side of the enormous labels typed 'GLUCOSE' in big, bold letters. It was truly amazing to think that it was here that the phenomenal magic of sweet making began for this shop.

She explained that the equipment on the work surfaces where for grinding fresh sherbet. On another surface, she pointed to three great walloping pots. The heated pots stirred silky, warm chocolate in a constant cycle through its system of pipes with chocolate running taps overhanging the basin. One for smooth sweet milk chocolate, another with rich glossy dark chocolate and finally creamy white chocolate. "I make all of my own chocolate work here too. Easter Eggs, Christmas liqueur chocolates, valentine boxes and our best seller is these chocolate frogs” She pointed at a tray full of peppermint chocolate frogs. They looked amazing.

“I would give my arm to hover underneath those taps, and slurp melted chocolate straight from that tap.” I said, and she nodded seriously, as if she believed me.

Alongside the wall stood a huge stainless-steel metal table. It had lots of buttons, knobs and nozzles on a control panel. A large heat lamp perched over the top covering most of the table area. It was held on by a long electrical cord hanging from the ceiling and swung wherever you wanted it to go. "And what is this for?" I pointed and asked in awe.

"That is a heated table. I pour the sweetie mix onto the table after the sugar has boiled to the temperature I need. The table is warmed from below and the lamp heats from above. It keeps the mixture warm so that I can work with the mixture for longer so that it doesn't set solid before I move it through the next machine. It buys me a lot more time so that I can add colours and flavours to the boiled sugar. If I put the boiled sugar on a cold table, the sugar mass would set hard very quickly, and I would be left with a humbug big enough to feed a giant. Most of my customers are human; not all, but most. Therefore, I tend to cater for them in smaller bitesize pieces."

Imagine that I thought! What if some of her customers were really giants? My mind whizzed. At least they could get hold of suitably sized confectionery!

It didn’t take a lot for my mind to wander as you may have observed.

"It's jolly tricky to get right and very easy to get wrong, you must know precisely when to put the mix through the roller, or you will seize up the machine. Which at the worst will break the machine but at best leave you chipping off sticky sweets for half a day!”

In the middle of the floor stood the said machine that very much looked like a large clothes mangle. The kind that a Victorian housemaid would have used in the olden days to wring out wet clothes. I couldn't imagine that that was what its purpose was. The room didn’t really lend itself to laundry. I stared and pointed...

"Whatever is that?" I asked with still a gob full of more delicious pips, trying but failing to slow down my consumption. Somehow knowing she had made them, they seemed even more enjoyable.

"That, my Dear I am getting to. It is called a drop roller. Marvellous bit of kit that I could not live without. After the sugar has been boiled to a high enough temperature, then flavours and colours have been added, I make a large patty. Then I must squeeze and feed the sugar patty through those rollers. Then the rollers turn and press the patty into small bite-size sweetie shapes." I looked a little closer at the rollers and inside each roller was an indent in the shape of a heart. I smiled with delight.

"These are for making my heart-shaped chocolate limes. One of my all-time classic best sellers and a recipe passed onto me by an old lady with bright red hair that I knew as a child." She beamed with pride.

"I use lime oil that has been pressed on a beautiful farm in Italy, and the chocolate comes from my friend, a hilarious chap in Belgium I met years ago.

'How remarkable' I thought. The story of where the ingredients come from alone would be interesting enough.

She switched the machine on with great excitement to show to me it in motion. The rollers spun around at speed with a very tiny gap in between. The sweets would be fed through the rollers and squashed into shape. When the perfectly shaped sweets came out of the other end still slightly warm, they were then fed onto a small conveyor belt. Over the top hung a cooler fan to quickly blow cool the warmed sweets as they slowly rolled by. It was exceptionally noisy, so she switched it off. I got the impression she was very proud of her machine. She had travelled to Kashmir in India to purchase it herself. It was too big to bring home, so she had it shipped to the sweet shop on a large wooden pallet. It was her pride and joy, and you could see that much. She pointed to the great selection of rollers with all sorts of shapes. It was terrific to see spheres for fruit balls, squares for cola cubes, ovals for humbugs and my favourite tiny pip shapes too.

“I have made a zillion mistakes over the years and gotten myself into very sticky situations with the hot, tacky stuff. It takes years of practice." she proclaimed. I felt quite privileged to have had a personal tour, but a new customer had just entered, and it was high time I went back to work.

I thanked the lovely lady. She, in return, thanked me for my interest and told me her name was Granny Bubbles.

It was time for me to make my way back to Mr 'happy' Plums. I was rather wishing afterwards that I had been sensible and maybe had a sandwich for lunch. The pips were starting to make me feel giddy with a sugar rush. I was delighted that I had broken my mundane day and witnessed sweetie making of a real-life confectioner. It cheered me up no end.

A few days later during my lunch break, I popped back into the shop for another round of moreish cola pips. The smell of vanilla beckoned me in quicker. When

I entered, I heard a yell from the back room. "Hello Dear!!!" she yelled from the kitchen. "I'll be with you shortly." Granny Bubbles voice sounded a little higher in pitch and slightly panicked. "In fact," she yelled quickly "I don't suppose you could help me?"

She was having a spot of difficulty with a batch of Devon cream fudge. Her assistant had just popped to the sandwich shop at that critical moment when she needed help lifting a hefty batch. All hot and flustered she puffed "I just need you to pick up that oven glove and help me lift this copper pan by the handle so that we can transfer it over to the warming table?"

A selection of trays laid out for fudge pouring was set out on the table. "We need to pour the hot fudge into these trays, be careful. It's very, very hot!".

With every ounce of concentration and trying to avoid the steam from fogging up my glasses, I helped move the colossal copper pan over to the awaiting trays and began to assist her pour until the copper pan was utterly empty. Granny Bubbles scooped out the remains with a giant spatula leaving nothing behind but a thin coating of the delicious smelling fudge.

Granny Bubbles let out a sigh of relief. "Thank you so much Dear!! I don't know what I would have done without you. Are you on your lunch break?"

"I am." I chirped.

"Well let me get you a cup of tea, and I have just made some fresh mushroom soup. We shall eat it together. You can have a bag of cola pips after your lunch as a thank you, but you must have something nutritional first, or you'll be giddy when you go back to work."

How could I possibly refuse? We sat and chatted for so long I got into trouble with the mouldy old plum for being late, but I didn't care. I was gripped in conversation with this fascinating lady who had many exciting tales to share with me. From then on, we became firm friends, and she told me all the Gobstopping Gossip of the shop and all about her adventures and how she came to be.

Chapter Three

Strawberries and Geese

Granny Bubbles was a plump lady with neat white salt and pepper curls, which she scooped up in a large hair bun on top of her head. She was a young grandma, not quite old enough to sit in a rocking chair knitting, complaining about potholes or dog poo on the pavement. She had a very polite manner with a rumbling hint that commanded some respect. Kind, and gentle but not to be messed with either.

Her skin tone was like an English cream rose with a smooth complexion, with a few hairline wrinkles.

She was not a sun worshipper and never had been, so her skin was in relatively good nick for her age. She had permanently flushed pink cheeks and her eyes sparkled grey with a hint of a yellow hue around the black pupils. They were framed with long black eyelashes, and she wore small silver metal-framed glasses perched on top of a charming button nose. Ladies' noses often grew larger as they got older, but Granny Bubbles had been lucky enough to escape this.

Her figure could have done with a little work in all honesty. She was apple-shaped with slender arms and legs and a podgy belly wrapped around her middle. A little bit like a potato with cocktail sticks for arms and legs. Well, not quite but you get the picture.

It was not what she had wanted for her vessel through adult life but if you choose to put everybody else's needs first and then choose a confectionery career with an added dislike of intense exercise, then something must give. In Granny Bubbles' case, it was her belly! But there was just more to cuddle, and she didn't have time to worry about her appearance, she had far too much to do.

Granny Bubbles' wardrobe was limited to simple black polo neck jumpers, black trousers and comfy shoes. Luckily this would all be smothered with a large chocolate brown apron which nearly always had bonbon dust and toffee drippings all over it. It is rather hard to keep neat and tidy in a sticky sweet shop, but this suited Granny Bubbles. She didn't need to be beach ready in her line of work.

Before she was married, her name was Violet Rose Valentine. As a girl, Violet Rose had grown up on a beautiful farm in the sunny south of England. The winding gravel road to the farm was edged with Bramley apple and Conference pear trees either side, which blossomed in spring and looked like a blanket of snow. The goats loved to graze the fallen petals and then the overripe fruit in the autumn. If they were too ripe and had fermented, then the goats would be drunk. A drunk goat is quite a sight. In the summer, the trees were crammed with delicious fruit—the farmland comprised of acres and acres of various fields, each growing different crop.

Dry brown muddy fields were lined with straw as far as the eye could see. Perfect rows of green strawberry plants uniformly embedded in the soil. This is where the name STRAWBERRY comes from. Berries that are grown amongst the straw!

The raspberry thickets were plump and plentiful, full of tiny blossom or fruit depending on the time of year. A border of blackberry bushes caged many of the strawberry fields. A field dedicated to the busy honeybees that feasted off the fruit blossoms and produced the most amazing floral sticky sweet honey.

A clowder of cats patrolled the fields for mice, birds and snakes. These feline police hid in between rows and thickets to keep the fruit safe from being eaten by the pests. They were like a fierce army of fruit guardians. And a fantastic job they did too.

Violet Rose's great grandfather had built the farmhouse from scratch as a project to see if he could make a whole house instead of just making bricks. The traditional family business of brick making had gone back many generations. The farmhouse was large and very elaborate indeed. It was a Victorian red brick building with dark green ivy creeping up the sides and smothering some of the sash window edges, crowned at the front with three white ornately carved wooden fascia, framing the front-facing roof with three pitches. It was an unusual colour at the time of building, as all the other village houses were made from sandy coloured building stone. Great grandfather was merely experimenting with a new brick design, and the results were magnificent.

It was a very proud house and had been a perfect family home. But in the end, her grandfather didn't fancy farming very much. He wasn't very green fingered and turned most of the crops crispy brown. He also failed to keep the essential livestock animals alive! So, he decided it was best to stop farming and left the farm to his son Arthur. He could then continue with the brick making. It was in everyone's interest. You couldn't kill a brick, you see!

A berry red door with fancy stained-glass panels and a brass letterbox sat proudly in the house's centre. Welcoming everyone in for any amount of fantastic cooking, whether they wanted it or not.

Violet Rose's mother Louisa was quite a feeder and thrived off catering for as many folks as she could humanly feed. There was always plenty of food to go around with much of it made or grown on the farm. Inside the kitchen, folk warmed up by the giant black wood-burning oven stove. The stove oven served a few purposes. It was used for cooking on as well as heating the downstairs quite handsomely. Washing would dry in front of the stove, and the dogs parked up to warm their chilly snouts too.

Louisa could not let anybody go hungry in her presence. At a minimum a cup of tea or a glass of raspberry gin was issued on entry followed by a cheese scone. "No" was not a word that would be understood. You would receive a feed whether you liked it or not.

Every day family and guests sat at a long wooden table with extended benches either side to accommodate many, many people. At each end perched two wooden thrones made by the farmworkers one year, as a 'thank you' present after the season had ended. They were like one big happy family. At any breakfast, over twenty people could be at the table. There would always be piping hot tea in the pot, fresh fruit, fried eggs and wholesome crusty loaves baked every day smothered with golden honey. Louisa Valentine took it upon herself to ensure all the family and farm workers had full bellies before they started work each day. She would prepare a huge pot of soup for lunch too. She lived to feed people and farm animals.

There was a hierarchy amongst the animals on the farm. The ill-mannered white geese and speckled brown chickens pompously wandered freely, pecking at scraps and bugs on the land and occasionally terrorising the dogs, especially if they came too close to their food or sometimes just for fun. Then the dogs would feel the wroth of a sharp beak.

These geese were not to be trifled with. They certainly had a superiority complex and ruled their turf with military precision. The geese were called Lucy, Lois and Neil. Interestingly Neil laid eggs too. But it was far too late to change her name to a female one by the time anyone had realised. It rather suited her anyway, she was the self-proclaimed leader, and Lucy and Lois did as they were told.

At night, many stragglers from the village pub often became lost on their way home, crunching up the gravel drive and ending up entirely lost up the farm track. Neil would soon chase them out! Sobering the drunks up reasonably quickly, a nip from Neil would see to that. The geese made much better guard dogs than the actual dogs.

The two dogs were at the bottom of the farm's pecking order. Probably under the rats that the cats caught. They were cocker spaniels whose primary mission in life was to try with all their might NOT to expend any energy more than necessary. Arthur's error was when he accidentally bought 'Show Cocker Spaniels' instead of 'Working Cocker Spaniels', quite different breeds entirely. Show cockers are companion dogs bred for beauty and affection and working cockers, well, work! A schoolboy error that would cost Arthur a good fifteen years of intense fussing and petting. Quite useless to a farmer. They didn't really come to attention until there was a rustle of a food packet or the sniff of cooking. They stationed themselves on the mat in front of the oven. Mostly to keep warm but also to be as close to food as possible during the daytime. In the evening, they perched on anybody's lap who'd take them and snuggled in for warmth and affection. They were very loveable but utterly useless, outrageously lazy and selectively deaf. They did win a few rosettes in dog shows for best of the breed. But never for agility!

Neither the dogs nor the geese would take on the cats though. Cats ruled this farm, but then they did such an excellent job of protecting the crops, that their wicked conduct was tolerated by all. It is thought that the cats knew they COULD get away with bad behaviour and did so. They regularly became cross with each other for no apparent reason, but worse was if YOU were in the wrong place at the wrong time. They would sneak up on you in the dark and claw your legs, giving you quite a fright for absolutely no reason. It would not be unheard of for a cat to cosy up to you and lull you into a false sense of affection. Then in a flash an unjustified claw slash or a blatant spiteful bum hole display too close to your face. They were not kind beings, but they served an essential purpose, and that was how it was.

The farm was truly a great place to grow up. With fresh air, space and freedom alongside learning to graft hard and learn a sturdy work ethic, which was instilled into Violet Rose from the start. There was no better place to be. But it wasn't all strawberries and fresh cream!

Chapter Four

Spiders and Jelly Boots

Violet Rose Valentine had an idyllic childhood, with long summer days, helping her parents and siblings, grow and pick the sweet strawberries, bright red raspberries, juicy blackberries and tangy gooseberries.

The mountains of produce would be weighed, driven by lorry and sold to the Jam factory a few miles down the other end of town. These people bought fruits from many farms and made jam for the whole country, including the King and Queen of England. On the side of each jam jar, it displayed a royal crest. As Violet Rose picked, she daydreamed that the fruit she had gathered may have graced a royal crumpet or perhaps a hot buttered scone? It gave her great pride to think she was doing her bit for her country.

Her father, Arthur Valentine, paid her pocket money for all the fruit she picked, which burned a hole in her pocket. Much of this money was spent on 'Mr Swans' the local newsagents in the village. Mr Swan always stocked her favourite fruit pips and bazooka bubble gum.

Whilst picking the fruit she would stuff her chops with as much bubble gum as she could load in to blow pink bubbles the size of her head. The bigger, the better. Quite often she would get into such a pickle after the bubbles would burst into her curly fringe and stick onto her spectacles. Her mother would despair at all the sticky mess, and afterwards, she would have no option but to cut the bubble gum out of Violet Roses hair with scissors leaving her hair with awkward spikes poking out of her pigtails.

The more Violet Rose practised, the better she got at calculating the moment of eruption, sucking it back in before a disaster struck. It was the farmworkers who nicknamed her 'Bubbles'. Quite often they brought her extra bubble gum supplies so they could have bets at break times on how long she could keep a bubble alive or how big she could blow them. It was a useless talent that served no purpose at all. But it was what she enjoyed doing, so who was anyone to argue?

Violet Rose had grown up with two older brothers. Vincent Grape Valentine and Victor Victor

Valentine. These two pinheads were none-identical twins. One had a shock of wiry ginger hair with a handsome round face, blue eyes and a big conk for a nose. The other had dark brown curly hair, with dark brown eyes and was also handsome (if you liked that kind of thing, supposed Violet Rose). Victor was the oldest by three minutes and let Vincent know it most days.

Violet Rose's mother, Louisa, had left the naming of her children to her husband, Albert Valentine. A jolly, but firm man who worked extremely hard and expected everybody else to do so too. Vincent got the middle name 'Grape' because of a spelling error at the birth's registry office. It was supposed to be Grant but by the time Albert realised it was too late to change it. So,

Grape stayed as his middle name. Victor’s name was unusual too. Victor was named after Albert's father and his favourite cousin. Not wanting to leave either of his two favourite men out, he decided to call him Victor Victor Valentine.

Vincent and Victor had no other purpose on earth other than to create trouble. What havoc one didn't think of, the other one would.

The twins gave Violet Rose excellent grounding to stand up for herself in the future with anyone who tried to take her on. Whilst looking fluffy and cute, inside she was as hard as an iron bar on a cold day. She was never going to tap out of any attempt to get the better of her. She could be a Houdini and was quite used to getting herself out of sticky situations in a flash.

This was unwittingly the character her brothers had helped to create.

A common form of torture was a lengthy chase from the twins around the farm. A very vocal squealing Violet Rose was quite often caught in pursuit and would be pinned down by both twins so they could hover huge dripping ropes of snot over her face whilst she yelped in disgust.

She wriggled like a caught worm, hell-bent on making her mother hear her discomfort via ear-piercing screams. The boys howled laughing, just sniffing the stringy green snot back up before it slowly dropped too far-down. They knew Violet Rose would create merry hell if that snot had touched her and they knew their mum would punish them for being so utterly despicable. So, they just stopped short of their vile actions right before they knew they could be reprimanded.

Their mother would scold them with what some in society would consider a very peculiar parenting practice by sending them directly to the 'Lady with the Red Hair'.

The lady with the red hair was a withered looking hag who lived in a wonky old cottage on the edge of the farm grounds. It was a very dark, shadowy thatched cottage that had long needed a new roof. It sported thick green moss, blanketed all over its straw roof with patchy areas where the birds had raided the straw to build their own nests and the squirrels lived quite happily. It sat neatly in the shade of some very tall pine trees. No light ever seemed to reach it. Inside were bare floorboards and a small wood stove that burned all year round. The cottage always had an icy chill about it even in the height of summer.

It was her job to look after the twenty-five cats that controlled the rats and birds from eating the farm fruits. In return for her free cottage. She was an important part of the farm eco-system and at the same time a complete mystery to folk who didn't know her. Rumours that she was a witch and boiled up naughty children spread through the primary school like wildfire for generations. Parents passed down the stories that she caught bold children and kept them locked up.

It was somewhat a smelly home, as stinky as you would expect a cottage shared with twenty-five feral cats would be. But the lady was always smiling and polite, and for some reason had a shock of Red London Bus coloured hair. People only knew her as 'The Lady with the Red Hair'. Nobody knew her real name.

She LOVED seeing the farm children and often gave them a huge hug. This would have been quite ok had she not had a hairy lady chin that prickled you when she tried to kiss your face. It felt like an electric shock. She smoked roll-up cigarettes regularly, and she ate garlic bread with raw onion rings for every meal, so really had the most horrible stinking breath too. When she opened her mouth to smile or speak, the smell would bowl you over and take up the entire room. You Did NOT want a hug from 'The Lady with the red hair'.

She didn't care a jot for personal hygiene and would seldom shower, brush her teeth or brush her hair. She was quite a sight. The boys had a morbid fear of being in her presence as all silly boys would be. If they had been incredibly naughty, their mum would send the boys down to fix something, do an errand or take a freshly baked cake to her. She would be so gracious she would want to shower them with as much affection as she could. The boys LOATHED it and often gagged at the smell of her rancid tangy armpits. But the lady with the red hair was the only person that Louisa could use as a deterrent for their vile behaviour.

"That's it boys... if you don't behave you will have to take this cake down to the lady with the red hair".

The boys would freeze in horror. "No, no, no, Ok Mum, we will be good, we promise," they would plead in tandem. It did the trick and quite often made them fall back into line immediately. It was all she had, but it was all she needed for instant discipline.

Violet Rose was an unforgiving sole and would get her own back on the boys by dropping spiders in their soggy open mouths whilst they were asleep. One time she painted Victor's toenails red whilst he was napping in the hay, and when he found out, he chased her all over the farm. She refused to give him some nail varnish remover until he'd apologised for cutting off her pigtail curls whilst she was asleep the night before.

Once after a long day on the farm, she fell into bed exhausted. When she put her head on the pillow to fall asleep, she felt a rustle and a squeaking from inside the pillow. She, threw the pillow across the room, shot out of bed and shrieked in horror when she realised what it was. She was livid and vowed to get him back.

Vincent was treated to a boot full of jelly after he had placed a family of field mice in her pillowcase. When he put his feet in his only pair of boots, bright red raspberry jelly squished out every hole. He was furious and hurtled after her until his heels hurt from rubbing.

"I am going to smash you to a pulp Violent Rose, you better make sure you can outrun me!" he yelled in a rage.

Violet Rose was smart enough never to get caught by her mother for her crimes, so her halo always seemed to remain intact. A few times she even ran to the lady with the red hairs house knowing full well they wouldn't be able to catch her in there.

She really didn't mind the lady with the red hair. Having terrible hay fever as a child, quite often she had virtually no sense of smell. To Violet Rose, the lady with the red hair was just kind, a bit scruffy but had a nice heart. She spent quite a bit of time in the dark cottage as she grew up. Never actually calling her by her name because she didn’t know it and nor did anyone else!

Violet Rose attended the local village school, whereby she was naturally academic. Much to the disgust of her nemesis Lynn Jones-Jerms.

Lynn was a foul-tempered child who terrified everyone around her. She was very fussy about almost everything and had an opinion on everyone. She terrorised her parents with unreasonable demands and hated anyone more talented, creative, prettier or popular than her, which was pretty much everyone. This fact made Violet Rose a considerable target for Jones-Jerms. But Jones-Jerms had underestimated Violet Rose greatly, her steely determination and iron will to irritate with reverse psychology or by killing her with kindness. It was quite a weapon. She would be so kind and polite it would almost send Jones-Jerms into a fury at the sight of Violet Rose.

No matter how hard Jones-Jerms tried, Violet Rose would not bite. Violet Rose was taught that bullies and nasty people generally did not LIKE themselves, so they would see fit to take it out on the loveliest people to make themselves feel better. They were to be pitied, not feared.

She was also sharp enough to know that it annoyed Jones-Jerms much more not to get a rise out of her. The boys indirectly and accidentally taught her to fend for herself, and there was absolutely nothing Lynn Jones-Jerms could do that Violet Rose couldn't handle.

Chapter Five

Sprats and Ghosts

Violet Rose's best friend was called Clarabell. Clarabell was a kind girl, and the two of them had a common dislike for nasty pupils.

They spent much of their time plotting secret acts of revenge on baddies who had been mean to goodies. There was an occasion where Jones-Jerms had snatched a ruler from the sweetest boy in the class. She teased and tormented him to distraction. He was so upset and didn't have the life experience to deal with her vile behaviour. He was an only child and had never really had to fight for anything in his life, so he generally cried at the least little thing. Still, he was so lovely he would give you the shirt off his back if he thought you needed it. She waved the ruler around, and it made him very upset. He burst into tears and told the teacher. When he had walked away from the teacher's desk, unbeknown to him, Jones-Jerms had snuck the ruler back into his back trouser pocket. Deliberately making him look like a liar and a cry baby. Not only had he been humiliated, but the poor fellow also had a telling off by the teacher. He was a very sorry sight indeed. Jones-Jerms was smirking at his misery. It was just what she wanted.

Clarabell and Violet Rose had seen everything that had happened. They took him aside to try to stop him crying and vowed to get that bully Jones-Jerms back.

When Jones-Jerms wasn't looking, Clarabell sneaked into her lunch box and swapped the cheese slices in her sandwich for a wad of yellow paper post-it notes. Clarabell had written in her best scrawl:

'Be kind to all people,

or we will haunt you!!!!!!!!

From The GHOSTS'

Jones-Jerms was so looking forward to her lunch and was horrified after taking a big greedy bite of her favourite cheese sandwich. She spat out the imposter cheese slice and read out the message. If she wasn't raging before, she most certainly was now. For a moment, she silently fumed. Her eyes were as wide as saucers and to tell the truth, she was a little shaken. She did not know whether to scream with rage or cry with fear. What if the notes were really from ghosts?

To make matters worse, she confidently opened her can of Vimto that Violet Rose had previously shook up with every ounce of energy she had. Jones-Jerms jumped when she heard a bang and whoosh; it sprayed all over her face. Worse still, it dyed her white school shirt and pigtails purple for the rest of the day.

The other pupils who had been bullied by Jones-Jerms took the opportunity to laugh out loud, and they pointed at her, just as she had done to the poor boy and many of them.

You would have thought she may have felt a little embarrassed after now knowing just how it felt to be humiliated. But instead, Jones- Jerms was as angry as a raging badger and after blood. She VOWED if she had found out who was responsible, she vowed a lifetime of despicable things would happen. While all the time in the back of her mind, she thought the threat still might be real ghosts and that she might indeed be haunted.

It wasn't long before she was seen foraging in other people's lunch boxes stealing food and generally being a pest. Clarabell and Violet Rose were disappointed, but not surprised that it had ended up being a fruitless exercise. Their efforts wore off faster than they had hoped, but there was always next time. This was a long-term project to tame Jones-Jerms. Her ill behaviour was surely not sustainable?

On another occasion, Mr Wallops, the old Chemistry teacher, unfairly scolded a new girl for wearing the wrong colour socks to school on her first week. She had only been at the school a few days and had been trying ever so hard to get used to the new school rules and ways. Everything was new to her, and the poor girl was very nervous about making a mistake. Unfortunately for her, she could not have had a worse teacher than Mr Wallops. He was a mean man that revelled in telling children off and better still making them cry. He was quite hateful. Violet Rose and Clarabell did not like him one bit.

Mr Wallops was as bald as a swede, had a very smelly cigarette waft about him, stinking fish jumpers and rancid coffee breath after each break time. He wore a ghastly brown suit and wacky coloured socks, probably to make himself appear more attractive. He sported pointy leather tan shoes that looked far too big for him and like something Rumpelstiltskin might wear. He was very insensitive to anybody who made eye contact with him. Even the Head Teacher was nervous at the sight of his least favourite colleague.

Mr Wallop's had a hostile voice that boomed and bellowed all over the school. You would hear him before you could see him. As I said, he was a chemistry teacher. But pupils to precisely learnt nothing from him. He would settle the pupils into strict silence to copy from books all lesson and every lesson. Only raising his head to make a nasty comment or spit rancid drool over the unfortunate classmate at the front. He was always far too busy reading his fishing magazines. (Fishing was his life's love.) Which might explain the fishy-smelling jumpers.

He made every single man, child and beast dislike him. Not a soul was untouched by his unkindness. He had made the mistake of enlightening Violet Rose that she had "Two clods for brothers and would fully expect her to be a clod also." This was not news to Violet Rose. She understood Victor and Vincent were indeed clods. But there is one thing about the Valentines, only THEY can say mean things about each other. Violet Rose's blood boiled.

Clarabell was none too keen on Mr Wallops either. He had called Clarabells father a lazy man, who didn't work, and he fully expected her to be as lazy also. This couldn't be further from the truth. Unfortunately, Clarabells father had just had his fingers broken after a horse had bitten them. He was a horse racing jockey, you see. So, he had to have some time off to recover. It was just the sort of weapon that Mr Wallops would use to make another human feel worthless. He was a very nasty piece of work.

So, you see, each of the girls had an issue with Mr Wallops, as did most of the school. The final straw was after they had discovered the new girl sniffling in tears in the toilets because he had been so vulgar to her. They had decided enough was enough, and it was time.

While Mr Wallops was on his stinky coffee break, the girls snuck into his classroom with a jar of fishy sprats, Violet Rose's mother had been saving them for the cats on the farm. They were quite ready for the bin, but the cats would generally eat them regardless. They were certainly not for human consumption!

The girls hatched their plan a few days before. They had given careful consideration to which way they would get rid of this smelly old cretin. It wouldn't happen overnight, but it was a genius plan that was sure to hoof the old goat out of school forever. While Clarabell kept watch outside, inside Mr Wallop's classroom, Violet Rose snuck over to the large window, where a set of long ugly tangerine drapes hung closed. Blocking the beautiful sunny day out of the room like they always did.

There was a lining hole at the bottom of the dreadful orange nylon curtains that ran the full width, just big enough to fit a consignment of stinky old sprats inside. One by one, Violet Rose pushed the small, crusty, silvery fish into the curtain lining like a tiny fish train reaching right to the very end. "Let's see how much he likes his fish now!" sniggered Violet Rose. The girls were very pleased with themselves.

Nothing happened for a few days... and then Bang!!!! Mr Wallop's classroom honked of a genuinely the foulest fish pong you ever did smell. Much, much fishier than his usual fragrance of 'L'eau du fish' on his filthy brown jumpers.

Each time he entered his classroom, for the life of him, he could not find where the dreadful smell was coming from. Day by day, it got far worse as the fish began to rot. He was so incensed by the smell he could take no more. Gradually he began stripping the entire room of furnishings, ripping it all apart, trying desperately to solve the mystery smell.

All the pupils knew precisely what was going on, but collectively they kept quietly amused at his distress. Eventually, he started to despise coming to school. Finally, when there was nowhere further to look for the smell, he angrily insisted to the Head Teacher that he move classrooms immediately. The Head Teacher agreed and found a free ground floor classroom, took all his files and books with him to his shiny new classroom and settled him into it at speed. He moved his desks and chairs, blackboard, books and finally putting up the curtains he had taken with him from his old classroom! The plan could not have worked out better if the girls had tried.

Eventually, he couldn't take the smell any longer. He was so enraged, he took it out on the pupils, his behaviour towards them grew far more aggressive and hostile by the day. If he wasn't foul before, he certainly was now.

The final straw was after he threw a boy called Rosario out of an open window, headfirst into the paddock outside. Rosario's crime was calling Mr Wallops "Billy the Fish" within earshot. The Head Teacher was summoned to the classroom.

"What is the meaning of this Mr Wallops? There was absolutely no need to throw Rosario clean out of that window. No matter how annoying he is. You could have broken his bones." yelled the Head Teacher Mr Moon in front of the whole class.

Mr Wallops was incandescent with rage. "I don't care if that little meat head breaks every bone in his body. I hate him, I hate them all, I hate this classroom, I hate this school, I hate your big fat, ginger head and your school stinks of fish." he barked with venom.

The entire class went deadly silent while Mr Moon's ginger head turned a furious shade of crimson

"MR WALLOPS!!!! YOU ARE FIRED. GET OUT OF MY SCHOOL AND NEVER DARKEN MY SCHOOL DOORS AGAIN" raged Mr Moon.

Wallops left the classroom with his parsnip head a fantastic shade of purple in a fury. He departed school in his fishing van and drove home as fast as he could. Usually, he would have tried fishing to calm himself down, but if he had caught a fish, the smell would have sent him back into a rage again. Finally, he knew how it felt to be belittled. Just like he had done to so many children. He was without a job, and it was all his own fault.

Fortunately for Clarabell and Violet Rose, Mr Wallops was replaced by the loveliest teacher called Miss Pepper. She immediately took the dreary curtains down and put fresh blinds up. She taught in a beautiful, sunny, happy classroom. The girls were delighted at the outcome.

Chapter Six

Bonbons and Bullies

Stanley Thuggle walked into the canteen with a swagger. Not even a good swagger. An overswing of his gangly arms and too big an open-legged stride that made him look like he had a rugby ball up his bottom. His legs were so far apart that a pig could probably run through them with ease.

He was large, ridiculous, loud and trying far too hard to be cool. He was, in fact, a testosterone twit and looked more like a trainee ogre. He was just too big to be ignored.

Gary Tweed was just about to take a bite out of his marmite and salad cream sandwich when Stanley smacked him clean on the back of his head causing his crustless sandwich to fly out of his hand and land in Helena's raspberry and lemon yoghurt. Both were very displeased with the situation. But instead of reprimanding him, they sorted themselves out quietly and picked apart the remains of their lunch.

Jones - Jerms was, for a change, quietly minding her own business when Stanley threw his school bag on the round lunch table, causing Jones -Jerms Vimto bottle to spill its contents everywhere. It had trickled off the table and soaked her bright white school socks purple. All her hard-earned bullying had acquired that drink earlier that morning. Now it was all dripping onto the floor into her bag too. She was livid. But not livid enough to stand up to Stanley. She quietly mopped it up and found a cup of water to drink instead. The labour of putting Stanley the meat head back into place just wasn't worth it. He was too thick ever to be wrong, so people had given up trying to reason with him. Most people feared his size and ability to make school life very miserable indeed. During a science lesson he once literally got away with murder. After breaking into the science safe cupboard, he put a small block of potassium metal into the goldfish tank which fizzed and spun over the water causing it to flame purple violently. Poor Finn the fish was blasted to death after the water in the tank caught fire. Finns floated to the top whereby Stanley reached in and put the dead fish in his pocket.

The whole class was sworn to secrecy, or they would be head dunked in the loo first, then headfirst in the sawdust bin in the Woodwork room!

His presence in the canteen was enough to upset pretty much everyone within arm's length. He was an animal. Too big for the size of his brain. Too big for any room with his lack of spatial awareness. Utter chaos wherever he went. He was like a giant toddler flailing around. Leaving mass destruction behind him, he eventually found an empty chair, pulled it out and slumped his enormous being down on it. He immediately eyeballed a small boy. Alex, who was seated opposite. Without a word, Alex slid his full lunch box directly over to vile Stanley.

Today Alex would be going hungry. He had learned from the last time he objected when Stanley hovered Alex's head over the toilet waiting for an apology for not surrendering his lunch quicker. Stanley was THE PITS.

Stanley tucked into Alex's cheese and pickle sandwiches, cheese and onion crisps and cheese triangles followed by a tiny pot of cheesecake. Stanley loved cheese, and it appeared to settle him for a moment. Like a hungry bear taking time out to not be grizzly for a few minutes. Everyone was relieved and relaxed that while he was eating, a snippet of calm would prevail. They each returned to a hum of chitter-chatter and packed lunch box rustling. For a moment, just a moment, there was peace. At least until he'd finished the cheesy feast that poor Alex's mum had prepared for her cherished only child.

Clarabell and Violet Rose were unfortunately for them, sat opposite Stanley on the round lunch table too. They were eating their lunch as fast as they could, keeping one eye on him and one on their food before Stanley could start sizing up their food too. Clara slipped Brett an apple and one of Violet Roses spare Strawberry Jam sandwiches. Violet Rose always had far too much; her mother would rather boil her arm in hot tar than see anyone in her care hungry.

Violet Rose had eaten most of her packed lunch but remembered she had a bag of Raspberry Blue Bonbons in her blazer pocket that she had bought from Swans on the way to school. She pulled out a full, red and white stripy bag. Just at that moment, Stanley caught her eye. She knew what was coming.

Stanley reached over the table in one fell swoop and snatched the stripy bag off her. "How good of you to buy me sweets" he snarled.

"I didn't!" Violet Rose protested. But it was too late, and the bag was in his hands now. She knew it was fruitless to fight back with this thick head.

"My absolute favourite" He drooled as he shoved a good five blue Bonbons in his massive mouth at once.

He chewed and drooled blue like a bulldog with dribble falling from his big fat swollen lips, looking Violet Rose straight in the eye for a reaction. He enjoyed being unkind almost as much as the Stolen Bonbons. He started to throw the Bonbons into the air and catch them in his big fat mouth. He was picking up speed each time and tossing them higher each time. Showing off and shouting out loud so the whole room would look at him.

Violet Rose stared at his face and thought to herself 'Wouldn't it be payback if he cho...." and just then, Stanley began to choke.

He had inhaled a Bonbon from such a height that it had gained enough speed to lodge itself deep in his gullet. As much he tried to shout, he couldn't. The air was neither going in nor coming out! Sheer panic began to flash through his beady eyes. His cheeks were turning pink, red ...

"Gosh!" said Clarabell, "he's almost as blue as your Bonbons Vi", she said in a calm, slow tone, that implied she had no intention of personally helping him breathe again.

A crowd began to form around him. They stopped and stared. Nobody seemed in a hurry to help him very much. He had burnt all his bridges with every pupil in the school, one by one mistreating them all. They helpfully agreed how similar indeed that blue shade his face currently was a close shade to that of the Raspberry Bonbons. He slowly morphed into a very odd shade of purple.

Violet Rose decided that this shade of purple head might imply he was quite close to no longer being alive. She wanted him to suffer a little bit, perhaps, but maybe not die. She felt a pang of obligation to be the one to help him. After all, they used to be her Bonbons, and it didn't look like anybody else was going to help. She stood behind his substantial chest, barely wrapping her arms around him, bent him over as far as she could and quickly pulled him into her with a sharp shock. She had learned this manoeuvre previously, when Vincent has swallowed a hungry hippo ball to win a game against Vincent who had HIS winning ball wedged up his nose.

With one massive whoop and cough, the large, congealed Bonbons mess dislodged from his airway and splatted on the floor in a pool of his blue saliva. It was a grim sight.

"Thank me then?" said Violet Rose.

"You saved me." whimpered the bully. He looked slightly green at this stage, sheepish and a little bewildered.

Violet Rose began to feel very uncomfortable. She had never seen Stanley in this light before. Not once had she seen any remorse or inkling of humanity. His normally grimacing face contorted into thankful expression. It was alien.

Violet Rose and Clarabell hurried out of the canteen not as quickly as their school shoes would allow.

Stanley began to cry. He vowed from that moment on that he was indebted to Violet Rose for saving his life. All the other children stared at him in disbelief, and a few brave people started to laugh and point at him crying. Stanley for once didn't even rage up. He just sat quietly, contemplating how close to death he had come.

From then on, if he was caught taking anybody's lunch or bullying any of Violet Roses friends. She would only have to look in Stanley's direction and he would stop immediately. Stanley was in Violet Rose's pocket for eternity. She was the only human on earth who could control him, and she used her powers for good.

She eventually helped to mould him into a much less horrid human. Her classmates were delighted, and Brett even put on a few pounds of weight after being able to eat his lunch without interference. It was an all-round good event.

Chapter Seven

Wheatblox and Cider Bellies

Granny Bubbles had ten children. Four girls and six boys. For quite some time, she had to raise her children alone. She was married, only once, to her husband and once was quite enough! She married Paddy O'Shrimpling.

It was utter fate that they had even met at all. Patrick O'Shrimpling or "Paddy" for short was born on the Emerald Isle, Ireland.

He was raised in a smart port town called Dun Laoghaire (if you are unfamiliar with the Gaelic Irish language it is pronounced Dun-Leer-ee,). Paddy had left school early, eager to earn money. His dream was to buy his very own racehorse. Paddy's mother and father were a team of milliner's making fancy hats for wealthy customers in Dublin city. Paddy didn't have a creative bone in his body. So, the family business was not for him.

He adored horses, though, they were his passion. There was nothing he couldn't tell you about any horse, especially racehorses like Appaloosa, Suffolk punch, Cleveland Bay, Warmblood, Hanoverian, Gelderland and Dutch warmblood. If you had him on the subject of shire horses, you had better settle in for the night.

For a few years, he had been working in the other family business with his Uncle O'Shrimpling at

'O'Shrimpling's Trap Makers'. These were not mouse traps or rat traps as you might imagine. These were a different kind of trap, for much larger animals. Horses! Perhaps you are now picturing a giant car-sized mouse trap with a carrot bait to catch horses? But you would be entirely wrong.

Assuming again, you are not aware; horse traps were two-wheeled carriages that attach to the horse for transport or racing purposes—a bit like a chariot. But sadly, for Paddy and Uncle O'Shrimpling, work had dried up. Other faster modes of transport soon replaced horses. Horse and traps soon fell out of fashion. Increasingly cars and trains had become the favoured mode of transportation, so this had put Uncle O'Shrimpling quite out of business. His uncle had suggested he take a trip into the city to find a new job, as he didn't have any more work for Paddy. He could stay with his aunt until he was on his feet.

Paddy soon found himself on the train heading for Dublin City to see about any suitable work to be had in the busy capital of Ireland. He daydreamed of riches. Working in a bank or maybe a person of the law might train him to be a fancy solicitor? Perhaps Paddy would find a job in a wealthy house and marry their rich daughter? There were a million things he dreamt he could do. But dreaming was probably all that was available to him at this stage. Paddy wasn't the brightest button in the box. Outside the equine knowledge, there was not much else to him. So, he was doubtful to become a wealthy professional. And without any substantial schooling to be spoken of, he'd be lucky to get a glass collecting job in a pub to start with. But it passed the time to dream, and fate would soon step in to help him.

It was a crushingly, slow train journey, and the train ride began to drag. He had run out of jobs to dream about and looked around for something to read. Quite by chance, a newspaper had been left on the train by an Englishman.

Paddy picked up The London Times that had been discarded on the seat opposite. Inside he came across a small job advertisement for a Farrier and stable hand. It was so little he very nearly overlooked the words that would lead to changing his life's direction in a completely different country forever.

As soon as he arrived at the Dublin City train station, he went with his gut feeling and called the number on the advertisement of the farm in the South of England. The job included accommodation, food and as much fruit as you could eat. It sounded perfect to Paddy. He dialled the English phone number, and a gentle voice answered. It was, indeed, Violet Rose. Neither of them realised at the time that it was their future husband and wife talking. She handed the phone to her father. In his confident, soft dreamy Irish accent, Paddy explained to the farmer why he was the man for the job. His extensive horse knowledge was second to none. The farmer liked the sound of Paddy and thought the horse experience would come in very handy on the farm, he gave him the job there and then over the phone. Paddy turned on his heels and was back on a train heading to the port with only his boat fare in his hand and just enough for some food. He set sail for England that same day, and within a few days, he was on the farm, set up in his room with food in his belly, ready to look after the farm horses. He couldn't be happier.

Violet Rose had no interest in this fine slim, tanned farm worker. Other girls in the village thought he was quite dreamy. She was mostly oblivious to his existence, and when she did encounter him, she found him annoying. To him, Violet Rose played very hard to get. She was far too busy with her studies to take any notice of boys. He tried everything he could to get her to notice him. Probably too hard. She always blanked him, but he liked a chase, and it only made him even more determined. Paddy was a firm fixture on the farm for a few years. He was an excellent worker, to begin with, but like most people, a good few years into a job, they tend to become complacent and less effective.

One day Paddy was in a terrible sweat and scampering around the barn in a panic. He had somehow lost the tractor keys in the haystack when he'd stopped for another unauthorised break. Violet Rose happened to be passing to fetch some corn for the chickens.

"Are you OK, Paddy?" Asked Violet Rose.

"No, Violet I'm NOT OK, I'm actually in a bit of bother", he said in his smooth but panicked Irish accent. She had never really taken much notice of him until that point, but her eyes where transfixed. His flushed cheeks and naivety seemed to make him glow. He was usually quite gruff and cocky, but he seemed a little softer in the dusty barn.

"What are you looking for?" asked Violet Rose.

"The tractor keys are in this haystack. Victor Victor moved a few bales around when I went for a tea, so I am not sure where on earth they are now. Oh, Violet Rose, your man will be giving out to me and sending me home on da boat if I can't find them!" he shuddered.

(Irish Translated- I think your father will have me fired if I can't find them.)

Violet Rose took one look around the barn and spied the keys immediately. It was a superpower she had to find lost items. When her brothers had misplaced things, Violet Rose could find them in a flash. But she wasn't going to tell HIM that. He always teased her relentlessly about all the reading Violet Rose did and that she would miss what was going on under her nose. But she loved to read. Her nose was always in a book escaping her world into far-flung adventures. It was far more interesting than listening to his nonsense at least.

Now was her chance to give him a taste of his own medicine and annoy him in return. Casually she picked up the keys and quietly put them in her pocket. She watched him sweat like a racehorse, his tanned head-turning shades of pink, red, purple to pale white.

Before his head burst into flames, she dangled the keys in front of him and ran to the other side of the barn, taking them with her. The colour ran back in his cheeks, and Paddy rugby tackled her by the lower of her legs into a bale of hay to retrieve them. Laughing loudly, he shouted in his Irish accent, "You bold girl, your father would have had me made into rashers."

(Translation – You are naughty. Your father would have had me made into bacon!)

Violet Rose was giggling so much her ribs ached. It was only then that she looked at him with different eyes. Perhaps it was because she was a bit older, now 17. He was a good seven years older than her but was more of a lad than a man. Before then she hadn't noticed his handsome tanned face and attractive smile. But up close, he suddenly seemed agreeable.

For many years he was fun and kind and made Violet Rose feel on top of the world and happy. She loved his stories from his hometown, and his Irish accent was easy on the ear to listen to.

She soon fell in love with him and one day after the last raspberry field had been harvested and it was time for Paddy to head back to Ireland; Paddy decided he didn't want to leave Violet Rose ever. He asked Violet Rose's father if he could marry her and stay on the farm.

Vincent and Victor didn't care much for Paddy O'Shrimpling because they knew he was too lazy when the boss was not looking and as much as her brothers could tease and torment their little sister, they each had a fiercely protective streak when it came to Violet Rose. But whatever they said to their father fell on deaf ears. Her father agreed to the marriage because Violet Rose always seemed so happy when Paddy was around, and that was all that was important to him.

After many years of courting the couple married in the local village church and had a considerable barn dance after the wedding, with everyone from the village and all the Irish relatives came to stay. Her brand-new husband had far too much apple cider, and he fell asleep in a prickly gooseberry bush. Violet Rose hadn't noticed his absence as she was far too busy enjoying dancing with her bridesmaids. One of them incidentally turned out to be Jones-Jerms. It is funny how things sometimes go full circle in life! In adult life, they were now very close friends and often laughed about their childhood feuds.

The wedding day turned out to be a huge indicator of how married life would be for Granny Bubbles in the future. But Violet Rose was a glass-half-full kind of girl and brushed any silly behaviour from him under the carpet.

Granny Bubbles and Paddy O'Shrimpling led a reasonably dull life. Her other superpower was breeding humans. Paddy only ever wanted one boy, but Granny Bubbles still wanted a girl.

After six boys were born, a girl was born then another three girls just in case any of the girls got lonely. She was a baby-making machine and revelled in it. She loved each one of them. It seemed the more children she had and the more love she had for them. For Paddy, this was quite the opposite of Paddy who grew more selfish, the more children that came along. He couldn't abide smelly nappies or tolerate baby noise. He did his level best to keep out of the way at work, and if he wasn't there, he was in the public house in the village.

Paddy's dreams of racehorse ownership slipped by year on year. He never really made it a priority to follow his plan and never saved enough money to pursue his dream either. The years went by, and Paddy took his failures out on his family. He was always a bit lazy, but now he made it his life's work to do as little as possible on the farm until Violet Rose's father finally sacked him. He had to find another job.

His lack of interest was so evident that he didn't even bother to learn his children's names. He called them "You" or "It". He'd often say mean things to them and make them cry. The children would run away if he were nearby. They didn't feel happy near their father, so learned to avoid him.

He wasn't a pleasant man anymore, nor was he funny any longer. His stories had all grown tired, and he wasn't even that clever. If he could be absent at home, he really would. He felt very hard done by having to share his life with eleven more people. Paddy grew ever more resentful and miserable.

In a bid to be away from his family, he frequented the local pub. His choice was "The Cat and Carrot".

Luckily Granny Bubbles received money for cakes and sweets that she made for a local bakery. So, she at least had some money for the children. It was a harsh existence for her, but she would, like most excellent mums, never let you know it. She kept the children fed, healthy, happy, clothed and warm all by herself. The children didn't want for anything.

Granny Bubbles had long fallen out of love with him. She was particularly good at ghosting people. It was a survival skill she had learnt early on in her life. If someone was upsetting her, she could ignore them and pretend they were invisible and that's what she did with Paddy.

By the end, Paddy had gotten obese from all the cider he drank every day, and his hair had all but vanished with only a grey dirty beard furnishing his face. Quite often the beard contained whatever food he had last eaten at the Cat and Carrot. His nose was misshapen like a bright red cauliflower on the end. It happened to people that had drunk too much alcohol. Paddy often came home very late in the dark after a busy day avoiding husbandly or fatherhood duties but rarely made it into the house. He was generally found fast asleep in the lavender bush at the bottom of the garden outside, having had far too much apple cider. Whereby Granny Bubbles would leave him, pretending she hadn't seen him. He was a hot mess of a man. Granny Bubbles would rather kiss a soggy wet fish than her husband. So, the lavender bush was welcome to him. Perhaps it would make him smell better?

The marriage ended abruptly one day after Paddy died. Granny Bubbles hadn't noticed for a while as she thought he might be in the pub or had taken up residence in the Lavender bush permanently.

He had worked at the cereal factory for twenty years after being fired from the farm and was due to receive an award for his lengthy service (even though he was the laziest, labour dodging worker in the factory, but his clocking in card told a different story). On the day he was due to collect his award it was rumoured that he had already visited the Cat and Carrot at lunchtime to celebrate, and he had swapped his cheese and pickle sandwiches for apple cider. He had a little more than was legal to operate machinery when he got back and his belly had gotten so large from all the apple cider, he had drunk over the years that while looking for his big wooden stirring paddle he misjudged the centre and then shot himself headfirst into the ferociously hot giant copper roasting vat. One minute he was there the next he was roasted in with the wheat! Nobody noticed for a while. He wasn't very popular at work because he was always too snappy and unkind. People tended to avoid him as much as they could. At lunchtime, he ate his lunch on a bench with his only work friend Errol. Errol was so hard of hearing from all the noise in his machinery department, and he couldn't make a word out of Paddy's dull conversations, so Errol didn't mind him so much.

It was only because Paddy's shoe had clogged up a tube in the Wheatblox system that anyone noticed he was even gone. Quite a grim death but at least it was quick, I suppose. The body had to be exhumed somehow, for it to be buried. But by that time, Paddy had been well and truly processed into those popular Wheatblox shapes and packaged into a yellow cereal box. So that is all that they had left to bury. Twenty yellow branded boxes of 72 Wheatblox megapacks lay in a coffin. It was quite a sight.

Luckily Granny Bubbles had the children who gave her all the love she would ever need. She didn't have a lot of time to dwell and be sad about his death, he was never around anyway, and when he was, he was neither use nor ornament. She had ten children to look after on her own.

Luckily Mr O'Shrimpling had life insurance which had paid off the house. Wheatblox felt so sad for Granny Bubbles that they issued her with a lump sum of money as compensation for Mr O'Shrimpling's death, even though technically it was his big fat cider belly that was to blame. The only loser in the event of Paddy's death was the landlord of The Cat and Carrot who cried into his empty till at the end of each night. Once the money at the Wheatblox factory had dwindled, it was time for Granny Bubbles to find ways to put food on the table and keep her two grandchildren and five children who still lived at home fed and watered! She had always kept the money for a rainy day, and this was a rainy day.

Chapter Eight

Thirty-Five High Street

Granny Bubbles needed a fresh start after the death of Paddy. She had always made cakes and sweets for her children. It was her superpower, producing treats as a currency that got homework done, bedrooms tidy and to clean their menagerie of pets out. Granny Bubbles children were like a plague of locusts when it came to food and treats. They could eat you out of house and home if you let them, especially the boys. One of her sons, Edward, insisted on not two, like ordinary people but six Wheatblox for his breakfast in the morning. Then again after his two dinners at teatime. Edward would think nothing of heading back to the cereal cupboard for an extra bowl of four or five more Wheatblox. It was a good job that Wheatblox had given the family a lifetime supply with the death compensation of Paddy. Edward was in tip top condition for Rugby. Giant in stature with muscly legs that would make a shire horse proud. You couldn't fill him up or make him fat if you tried. Rugby was his life, and he burnt a lot of the calories off while tackling and running around like a boy possessed. That may have been down to Granny Bubbles unique mode of parenting. Granny Bubbles had taught him to pretend that the rugby ball was his beloved, most favourite Bakewell Tart that his Grandma Louisa made him every other week. She told him to pretend that the other players were trying to steal it off him and that they would scoff the lot if they got hold of it. Nothing made Edward rage more than someone taking food away from him. It worked like a charm. All 6ft 4 of him would defend that Bakewell tart like a lion protecting his kill. He was one of the top players in the team.

Granny Bubbles would make a batch of chocolate and raisin cookies, and they wouldn't even get a chance to cool on the rack before the children had scoffed the whole batch. They were insatiable. She kept one step ahead of them all the time. Planning treats and food well in advance. Granny Bubbles children were not always easy to deal with. Growing up with Victor and Vincent had trained her to think ahead and always stay ahead of the game and that came in handy when lone parenting. Now that she was all on her own (but really, she always had been) she had to be smart.

The family lived within walking distance of a beautiful Victorian High Street and therefore within walking distance of every shop and service that a person could ever need. It was half a mile long with cobbled paths. Either side of the long High Street were beautiful ornate shop windows. The buildings were a uniform red brick Victorian style, with large glass shop windows from floor to ceiling, each pane decoratively framed in dark hardwood. The High Street had been relatively unchanged since it was built. The shops were beautifully crafted and lasted many, many years. Our High Street was probably like many around the country. There were butchers, bakers, cobblers, tailors, footwear, haberdashery, household goods, opticians, chip shops, stationers, carpet shops, curtain shops and cafes. The list went on. The one thing that was missing was the one thing that Granny Bubbles could plug the gap with.

It was here that Granny Bubbles had decided that her new choice in career was to be her lifelong dream to open a SWEET SHOP. She had thought about it even as a child when she used to blow giant bubble gum balloons.

It was now time to put her dreams into reality. She had a perfect visual inside her head of exactly how the shop would look, what she would stock and how the sweets would be presented.

In the middle of the High Street an extraordinary white-fronted bank stood proudly at the centre of the

High Street. Outside, it had two huge, towering wooden doors with the words "Bank" carved at the top. They were quite daunting to open as they were so heavy. Granny Bubbles pushed them open slowly and wandered inside. The bank greeted her with exceptionally high brilliant white ceilings with pretty wooden bosses crowned in the beams. It was a surprisingly warm place considering its size. It was welcoming, clean, warm and organised. Dark wooden floors and large oak and leather desks with smartly dressed bank tellers addressed the lines of customers coming and going. Taking money out and putting money in. It was a Monday, so it was hectic. Mondays were the day that all the High Street shop owners, pub landlords and business owners would deposit their takings to the bank. It was here Granny Bubbles requested a new account for her shiny new business. Luckily, she didn't need to borrow any money but did need a bank account for the new sweet shop.

The bank teller that Granny Bubbles went to was friendly and helpful. She was an attractive little lady with a warm smile. She stood out amongst the other tellers as they tended to pull concentrated faces and look quite grumpy. Her face was more relaxed. Granny Bubbles was pleased about that as she was a little nervous about people thinking she was as mad as a box of frogs for starting her new venture. Once Granny Bubbles had explained her plans, and why she needed a business account, the teller was more than excited to open her new account so long as she promised to stock

Lemon Bonbons. "NOT the chewy type that had too little lemon dust... they had to be the brown toffee flavour, coated in a deliciously zingy lemon powder that made your ears tickle at the thought of eating them."

Granny Bubbles knew what she was after and promised faithfully to stock them. It was the very beginning of Granny Bubbles Sweet Shop.

She left the bank with a tickle of excitement in her tummy. At the same time, with a great deal of fear at the unknown. The journey back home with the reality of her dream coming true was enough to make her feel giddy.

As she walked home through the High Street, she peered up and down. There were only a handful of empty shops, but one, in particular, caught her eye. It was perfect. The shop Granny Bubbles had fallen in love with was currently empty. It had already been a few different types of shops before Granny Bubbles had spotted it. The last shopkeeper had used it as a pet shop but had moved next door because the rent was cheaper. At first, she didn't like the thought of food being sold after all those smelly pets had been in the space. But Granny Bubbles had fallen in love with the magnificent arched windows at the front of the shop. It was an east-facing shop, which meant the sunlight would not melt all the sweets and chocolate in the middle of summer too. It was perfect. It didn't have a step at the door, which was vital for people who had trouble getting around. She had known this from her own Grandma, who refused to ever go into shops with steps. It was a lovely Victorian building with traditional red bricks. It had a vast thick metal white pole in the window which was used for water waste from the flats above, rather than leave it blank she decided to turn into a giant red and white candy cane.

The shop entrance door was a glass door with a hard-wooden frame and a fancy antique brass bell at the top that jingled every time it opened. It was just how she remembered her local sweet shop when she was a child. Just perfect.

A long glass counter stood at the rear of the shop. Granny Bubbles had made a firm decision to use this for the fudge display. She had made up her mind. 35 High Street was now going to be the new home of Granny Bubbles Sweet Shop and Giftware.

Granny Bubbles Sweet Shop
English Confectionery and Giftware
OPEN

Chapter Nine

Paint Brushes and Rum Balls

Granny Bubbles had found the perfect shop that she wanted, but to use it she had to agree with the Landlord, (who owned the shop) that the shop was to be occupied by Granny Bubbles in return for rent money and a deposit sum (just in case she missed a rent payment). She signed the agreement, once this was in place, the Landlord gave her the keys, and it was all systems go.

When she opened up and entered for the very first time, her imagination went into overdrive.

As a girl, she had always visited Mr Swans shop in the village for her bubble gum and pips. She had such fond memories of his shop, and she thought it would be only too fitting that it reminded her of her happy childhood when she used to visit with her pocket money.

Inside Mr Swans shop had been a large glass counter where he sold delicious crusty bread and dreamy creamy jam cakes. She used to press her nose up against the glass getting as close as she could. Quite often, Mrs Swan would ask "Violet Rose, darling ... please try to stop licking the glass. It is jolly hard to clean after your visits".

Violet Rose LOVED Mr Swans shop. It brought warm fuzzy sweet memories back as she pondered. The walls were smothered in warm wood panelling and had high shelves right to the top of the ceiling. Each shelf was rammed with all the goods you would possibly need in life on a daily basis. The stock looked like it went on for eternity because the shelves had mirrors at the back, which made it look like there was much more than there actually was.

35 High Street was already 102 years old and had plenty of charm and character of its own.

Before it was a sweet shop, it had been several shops. 35 High Street had been a Milliner's shop that sold fancy hats to wealthy ladies. It had also been a shoe repairer, mending men's leather shoes, a fancy soap shop selling high-end soaps and creams which later on became a national brand selling in all the posh department stores in London but had started from humble 35. It was also a cake shop that made beautiful wares that were transported down to London too to the Queen's grocers. So, it was a lucky shop.

35 High Street was a pet shop that had specialised in snakes, reptiles and all the creepy crawlies that they needed to feed upon. This thought gave Granny Bubbles the willies. When they were children Vincent and Victor had been hell-bent on terrorising Violet Rose with any spiders or insects they came across in the barns on the farm. They would collect them for this sole purpose, quite often tipping jar's full of them on her head in over her pigtails when she was resting. The terror would send Violet Rose into the stratosphere

with rage. The feeling of anything crawling made her shudder to this day.

Before a single sweet could reach the doors, it had to be thoroughly cleaned and painted from top to bottom. One morning while cleaning, Granny Bubbles had the fright of her life when a rogue cricket hopped into her ear. It brought back instant memories of her brothers' skulduggery. This little beast was quite obvious he was from the previous tenant's pet shop and had hopped out from a hole in the skirting board. She squealed, frantically brushing the little critter out of her ear. She was incandescent with rage and demanded to the pet shop owners that the crickets be removed immediately. The pet shop had moved over right next door at 33 High Street into a bigger shop where they could sell more and more and bigger creepy crawlies.

Apologetically the Pet Shop Man removed the hopping offenders, and he promised she would not see anymore. It turned out to be a VERY hollow promise, now and again a free-range Cricket or Zophobas Worm would grace her gaze. Each time she would scream the place down alerting Pet Shop Man to her despair. It was not a great start to their neighbourly relationship.

Glenda was a professional painter and decorator and was truly excellent at what she did. She had crazy wiry brown hair furnished with a dark denim train driver peaked cap. Glenda wore splatted white denim dungarees with every shade of the rainbow plopped on the front, back and sides where she wiped her brush clean and on her bum pockets too. She was not very feminine at all and not remotely interested in anything girly. This job and every painting job would come with a lengthy haggle and coax. If she had your ear space for more than a moment, it was sure to be filled up with complaints.

She would complain it was too hot or too cold. Glenda would complain that the painting job was too big or too small. She could be peevish about the colours that you had chosen, saying that they were too bright or too dull. She could be grouchy about the amount of time it would take her to do the job and often tapping her denim hat with her paintbrush as if that might make the job go away quicker. It seemed she would try to talk you out of even wanting the painting job doing in the first place. It was almost as if she didn't want to earn any money at all! Once Granny Bubbles had coaxed her in by the promise of cash, tea and her favourite Chocolate Rum Balls, she eventually gave in and got to work, beautifully brushing on the paint and cutting in (painting very straight lines without a ruler). Granny Bubbles knew it is tough to do, and she watched in awe.

The shopfront was smothered in the most delicious looking creamy chocolate coloured paint that was as close to chocolate colour as you could get. It looked good enough to eat.

35 High Street would then need a sign above the shop front if anyone were to know what delights were inside. She enlisted another old friend who was a traditional Sign Writer. 'Granny Bubbles Sweet Shop'

was emblazoned on a chocolate background with beautiful white block writing with a red and white candy cane snuggled through the middle of the crisp white letters. Underneath in smaller italic white writing said, 'Traditional English Handmade Confections & Giftware' You could see it from afar.

Glenda skilfully painted onto the door window in real gold leaf the opening times. The gold leaf twinkled in the sunlight.

On the two front windows emblazoned the crisp white painted wording. "Sweetie Hampers, Party Bags" on one pane and "Wedding Favours and Sweetie Buffets" on the other.

It was starting to take shape. Granny Bubbles was feeling warm and excited about it. Blossoming right in front of her eyes was her dream coming true.

Inside the door, the floor tiles were still the original century-old tiles. These were still bright white in a diamond shape with smaller black diamonds in the centre. Considering they had been there for over 100 years and probably had thousands upon thousands of feet walking over them in that time, they were in remarkable condition.

The walls were wood-panelled. The wooden shelves were the perfect size for glass sweetie jars. NOTHING else could fit in these spaces. Edward happened to be a trainee carpenter who had agreed to put up her shelving in return for sweets and tea too. It occurred to Granny Bubbles that sweets and tea seemed to get most things done and would keep this in mind for bartering for goods and services in the future.

A long glass counter was positioned at the back of the shop. So that customers had to walk past all the scrummy sweets before arriving at the till to pay. It was Glenda's idea. She was excellent at squeezing every last penny out of a situation for as little work as possible. In the centre of the shop stood another metal pole. It rose from floor to ceiling, just like the one in the window. To anyone else, this would have seemed it quite ridiculous to have large pole smack in the middle of the shop. Granny Bubbles decided the pole that kept the building structure in place would be painted crisp white, and then when that was dry, a twisted red stripe would make it looked like a giant candy cane in the middle of the shop to match the one in the window. It was rather fun and quite quirky. Rather than ignore them, it was best to make a feature thought Granny Bubbles.

With some shiny new light fittings, a glossy new till and sweet shop weighing scales, the shop was nearly ready. The one thing left was reasonably vital. SWEETS!!

Granny Bubbles had been stockpiling fudge, sherbet and coconut ice for some time. She had made all these in her kitchen at home. It was time for the most significant shopping experience of her life.

She had made an appointment with Mr Dean. He was the owner of the country's largest sweetie wholesaler. A wholesaler is someone who sells bulk items to people who break these items down into smaller portions to sell these items in their shops. A bit like a shop for shops! Mr Dean had a colossal warehouse stretching as far as the eye could see. The warehouse was stacked high with every sweet you could imagine. There were huge bags, and cardboard boxes in neat lines, high up to the ceiling on wooden pallets. Mr Dean was a clever chap. He bought from all the sweetie makers in the country and imported from around the world, every sweet you could imagine. He put them all in one place so that other sweetshop owners could buy sweets at a lower price for reselling at a profit. It allowed the sweet shop owners to visit just one site and give them a chance to make some money of their own, selling the goods on in their shops too.

The sweetie maker made money; Mr Dean made money then the sweet shop owner made money. If you are old enough to read this story, you are old enough to know that THIS is how the world goes around. Even if you are at the petrol station, the supermarket, the hat shop or buying trainers, THIS is how your shopping gets to you every time. It comes firstly from a manufacturer - wholesaler - to the shop - then to you, the consumer.

Granny Bubbles wrote a shopping list pages and pages long. On it was every sweet you could imagine, mints, liquorice, boiled, jelly, fizzy, lollipops, mega sours, pips, chews, white chocolate, dark chocolates, milk chocolates, chocolate covered nuts and raisins, toffees, counter sweets, foams, flying saucers, marzipan, creams, cough sweets and finally Sugar-Free sweets.

She worked through the list picking up huge 3kg bags of each type of sweets. If you don't know how big that is, it's enough to take 30 bags of sweets out.

Each section had a variety of flavours. The trollies began to overload and were piled so high they started to wobble. One after the other, after the other, was wheeled off to the till.

As this was her first shop; Mr Dean was very kind and gave her some money off her first purchases. It was essential to Mr Dean that his customers kept returning so, he did everything he could to help, and he intended to maintain a friendly relationship from the start. Granny Bubbles was pleased with the discount as it meant she could now afford a pavement sign. Once she had paid the mammoth bill, the staff helped her to the van and loaded up all the piles of sweets. Then she drove the long journey back to 35 High Street with a very heavy van indeed. She hoped she hadn't forgotten anything, and in her mind, she kept counting "Strawberry Bonbons, cola cubes, spearmint chews."

It was all very well shopping for a mammoth shop, but when she got back to the shop, she realised she couldn't unload it by herself.

Having ten children, you would have thought that at least one would have helped her, but alas they were all too busy with their own lives.

Enter Fabulous Alice. Alice was a schoolgirl in her last years who had been recommended to her by her brothers-wife's-friends-cousin-sisters-husband.

For someone so, young Granny Bubbles had lucked out when she met Fabulous Alice. She was a tiny girl with beautiful long brown hair and pretty grey eyes, which was an unusual combination but very fabulous. Fabulous Alice was a shy girl and would be crushingly embarrassed if complimented on her looks which made her all the more fabulous. She didn't have an egotistical bone in her body. All she was interested in was the job in hand and doing it correctly.

She was an absolute godsend. Often, she thought well ahead of time, attended to tasks without needing a prompt and generally being Granny Bubbles third hand. That was why she was called Fabulous Alice.

The van pulled up, and Fabulous Alice was waiting to be of assistance. She stood in her brand-new brown apron with Granny Bubbles Sweet Shop emblazoned on the front. It was her first day on the job, so she wanted to meet with approval. She had done a bit of babysitting, but this was her first real-life proper job. It was Friday night, and the big opening was Saturday morning. There was still a lot to be done, and a slight bit of panic began to set in! They unloaded the jars straight on to the shelves in order of the product. The Bon Bon flavours on one shelf, all fizzy jellies on another, a section for sherbet. Do you get the picture? Things needed to be easy to find and displayed sensibly. Granny Bubbles' daughter had suggested they show them alphabetically while her other daughter had suggested colour co-ordination. While that system may have worked for some people, at best it would look fantastic, but what if a customer was colour blind? So, they came up with a system of categories in the same area.

Before long the shelves were all filled up, the fudge cabinet was full of delicious homemade fudges, the counter sweets were neatly all in place, and the lollipop jar labels all aligned beautifully. The till had a cash float inside it for giving out change after a sale. Several sweetie hampers and party bag samples were displayed too. It looked a treat. They had worked so hard.

Finally, just before midnight, game on. Granny Bubbles Sweet Shop was finally ready for action.

Chapter Ten

Pythons and Parma Violets

Granny Bubbles had not slept very well at all, she had tossed and turned and had plumped her pillow up what felt like a million times. She tried to count sheep to get to sleep but just ended up counting sweet jars on shelves instead.

She was petrified she had made the wrong decision to open a sweet shop. People had told her that it would never work. Many people had suggested she was foolish to use the last of her inheritance money upon a vast stockpile of sweets. In reality, it *was* slightly bonkers.

She had a lot of doubt in her sanity and in her ability to pull this off. After all, what did she know about retail? Precisely zero was the answer. But in her heart of hearts, it felt like the right thing to do.

People's instinct is to fear change, and more importantly, how the change that will affect THEM. How your actions will affect THEIR lives was usually their objection. THAT is not a reason to NOT follow your dreams. That is why they are called "YOUR dreams". But she had learned along her life's path that if she had listened to every negative comment about her experience, nothing would have EVER got done. Sometimes you must be super brave, ignore the opinions of the people who sound like rabid parrots and be confident in your own choices and ultimately please yourself, and so she was. Albeit with utter terror in her belly.

All the preparation for the shop was now complete. It looked like a sweet shop, smelt like a sweet shop and on the outside, it even said "Sweet Shop". It was indeed a Sweet Shop. It was currently 4:30 am, and the doors were due to open at 9:00 am. It was the very first day that the shop was scheduled to begin trading. She was running out of sleep hours. She just could not settle. She tried with all her might to close her eyes tight shut and try and trick her body that she was sleepy. But it just would not work. She had uncomfortable knots in her tummy, and the muscles on her shoulders were so tight you could bounce a hammer off them. Eventually, she shouted to herself, “If I am awake, I might as well be up!" So, she slipped out of bed, got dressed and dashed off for a very early start.

When she arrived at the shop, she was surprised to find Fabulous Alice already there. Fabulous Alice was so excited she had decided to come in super early to make sure all the jars were polished and ready for display. Fabulous Alice had straightened everything up into beautiful lines so that all the jar labels were level and on the right way around. She had organised all the counter sweets in front of the till in perfect lines. The colours were a beautiful assault on the eyes. There were Wham bars, Highland Toffee bars, Rainbow Drops, Golf balls, Gob Stoppers the size of tennis balls, Refresher bars, Snap Crackle bars, cola, strawberry and cherry Fizz Wiz Popping Candy, Barratt Sherbet Fountains and Dip

Dabs all in neat rows, Wonka Nerds, Laffy Taffy, Love Hearts, and Parma Violets.

In the chocolate section, there were Fry's Creams, Caramac, KitKats and Bounty, the list went on and on. They all looked so inviting people were sure to buy them. But what if they didn't?

Fabulous Alice had tidied up all the rubbish and was just putting on the kettle when Granny Bubbles walked in. ' Was this girl sent from heaven?' thought Granny Bubbles. A final clean of the windows in the dark, it was still so early the sun was still yet to rise, a sweep of the pavement outside and a final floor clean inside the shop meant they were ready to roll. Only another 3 hours until opening to go but magically it all seemed to be in place and had come together. She had so much stock from around the United Kingdom, and beyond that, it looked more like an emporium than a shop. Granny Bubbles Sweet Shop, after all the hard work, was finally ready for business.

The pair sat together in the middle of the shop on some blue striped deck chairs and drank tea. It was quite peaceful to enjoy the shop alone for a moment while it was pristine and new. The calm before the storm if you like.

It was now 7:30 am. Opposite Granny Bubbles Sweet Shop sat a greasy spoon café called Mrs Crimble's Cafe. It had red plastic chairs and Formica tabletops with salt and pepper pots that looked like they had been used by a thousand people, for a thousand years. It was the type of café that looked worn out, but the food inside the relatively clean kitchen was home-cooked, wholesome and tasty. The smell of sizzling bacon wafted out the door. They were luring early start builders and tradespeople in for delicious hot food. It had been open for breakfast since 5:30 am, and the girls had watched people filter in one after the other the whole time. Granny Bubbles and Fabulous Alice locked up and crossed over the road to join the masses for breakfast. They ordered hot tea with crispy bacon sandwiches on fluffy white wedged bread from the local bakers with lashings of real butter from the local farmer and Heinz Tomato Sauce. It was a tasty breakfast, the perfect start to the day.

They sat in the window slowly eating, nervously wondering if anyone would come to the shop.

"What if not a soul comes?" said Granny Bubbles.

"I think I can bet my life we will have customers today." said Fabulous Alice.

"My mum, who is a school teacher said all the children at school had been talking excitedly about the new sweet shop opening all week. It was even mentioned in the church sermon this Sunday by the reverend, and the choir ladies were beside themselves!" Somehow Fabulous Alice seemed far more excited than Granny Bubbles, but then every penny in her life was not tied up in Drumstick lollies and Pink Nougat! Granny Bubbles was the most anxious she had ever been in her entire life. Even as a young lady when walking down the aisle to meet her new husband in front of the whole parish or even when she first gave birth, she could not remember being this nervous. It was all the money she had left in the world. It was the only thing she felt she was good at doing. If this didn't work, well, there was no plan B.

As they finished their delicious bacon wedgies and second tea of the day, they watched from the café, people gazing through the sweet shop window. Then more came, and more and before time as we Brits do so well, an orderly queue formed itself outside the front door. Granny Bubbles couldn't believe her eyes. It was now 8:50 am. They couldn't hide in the cafe forever. It was time.

They crossed the road and slipped around to the back door. Fabulous Alice switched the lights on and then the cash register. She couldn't wait to take her first sales in real life.

Granny Bubbles headed to the door and unlocked it slowly. She raised her voice to the long line of people and declared out loud to the crowd "Ladies and Gentlemen I present to you Granny Bubbles Sweet Shop. The finest sweet shop in the land is now officially OPEN.

She wedged the door open, and sensibly the queue wandered in perusing the magnificent range of confectionery. Before long, you could not see the floor for folk foraging, almost rabid for their favourite sweets. It was right then that they both knew that THIS was a GOOD idea after all. There was no time to relax.

Fabulous Alice was delighted with her first sale for 200g of Rose Turkish Delight and 100g of Pate de Fruit. She carefully weighed them out on the scales and put the Turkish Delight in a pink stripy bag then the Pate de Fruit in a yellow stripy bag so that the customer could tell the difference when they got the sweets home. The customer was a tiny, friendly older gentleman with a beige trilby hat and a matching colour rain mac on. He had a very kind smile. He complimented her on a beautiful shop and hoped he'd be back soon. As he walked away, Fabulous Alice noticed a cricket had jumped onto his trilby, but with a shop full of eyes, she decided to keep quiet.

It was a real buzz that a real customer bought real sweets and more importantly gave her REAL money in exchange. She was now in business.

Soon the shop was buzzing with locals, all pouring in to see the wares. Word had gotten out about the massive range of confectionery stock and one after the other they came. Chocolate peanuts, foam bananas, fruit chews. Stripy bag after stripy bag they sold. There seemed to be no pattern to the type of customers who came in. The old, the young, the tall, and the small. Everyone left happy and with a smile except for three unfortunate customers. They were seeking to buy Chewing Nuts. These were a strange confection of tiny hard toffee balls smothered in milk chocolate. These were neither chewy nor had they ever even seen a nut in their lives! Unfortunately for the sad three, the only machine in the world that made them had broken down and was awaiting a new part to be handcrafted by engineers in India. The machine had been in use for 65 years and occasionally did break down. But that made them even more unique and not to be taken for granted. Hopefully, it would be up and running soon she told them and promised to keep them posted. They were not very happy, but you can't please everyone!

The stream of customers continued all day. For some, all the excitement was just too much. A small boy had a rather massive meltdown in the middle of the shop. He decided the blue bonbons his mother had just bought him were now NOT what he wanted. Even though a few minutes before he had indeed said he wanted them quite happily, which was why his mother then paid for them. But unfortunately for the mother, on the way out, just out of the corner of his eye, he spotted giant jelly snakes. They were as long as his arm with a yellow jelly belly and swirly rainbow fruity body. Thinking he had done himself out of a great treat, he threw himself around the giant candy pole in the middle of the shop and refused to leave, clinging on as if his life depended on it. Desperately, she said he could have one next time, but this didn't seem to be the correct answer he was looking for. Arms and legs were kicking everywhere when she tried to prize him off the pole, shouting and crying with all his might. His poor mother was very embarrassed and wanted a hole in the floor to swallow her up. Instead of teaching him a lesson, she bought him the jelly snakes which released him from the pole. Again, Fabulous Alice rang the money into the till and popped the jelly snake into a red stripy bag and handed it over. For millisecond things were ok until the boy spotted some pink and white chocolate mice out the corner of his eye and the whole process started again. This boy was going to be ever so good for business, but it was excruciating to watch the poor mother just trying to keep calm amongst her utter crushing embarrassment inside. The more she bought him, the worse he got. Eventually, he left with more sweets than he knew what to do with. As he left, Granny Bubbles reminded him to make sure he brushed his teeth!

For the most part, the new customers seemed happy enough with their purchases and vowed to come back. Granny Bubbles knew that this was going to be the hard bit. It was getting folk to return for more. The sweet shop had become part of people's routine when they came to High Street each week. Time would tell if this was to be the case. But for today, ...it could be counted as a success.

It was a fantastic start to the business, and at the end of the day at closing time 4:30 pm, Granny Bubbles and Fabulous Alice were completely drained. It had been a very long day since bacon sandwiches in Crimble's. Neither of them had stopped for a moment all day. After the money in the till was all counted, providing there were no mistakes, it appeared that they had served 1326 bags of sweets. They had not anticipated such a start at all. The pair of them looked like they had been dragged through a prickly hedge by their feet. Their hair and makeup looked like it had been completed in the dark. Every step they took was a slow, delayed sticky step along a floor, smothered in squashed jellies, escaped aniseed balls and spilt sherbet. Each of their new aprons smothered in Bonbon dust, sticky fudge and sherbet residue all over themselves. Although, when they looked around the shop, apart from the floor, it didn't look like it had just had over 1000 humans through the door. The stock looked a little dented, but a quick straighten up, and it was suitable for the Monday trading. So, they quickly had a scoot around to clean, and they had finished.

Granny Bubbles had a black rubbish bag to put out in the backyard. She swung open the back door to the sight of the pet shop owner next door wrestling the with the tail of a 5-foot python on the brink of disappearing under his storage shed. She rubbed her eyes in disbelief and quietly closed the back door. She was far too tired to be alarmed, so brushed the vision under the carpet in her mind and pretended it hadn't happened. She was so tired, and there were no words.

They locked up and headed back to Crimble's Cafe for a sit-down and to have some oxtail soup. They hadn't eaten a thing all day, and it was all they could do to lift the spoon to their mouths. Granny Bubbles and Fabulous Alice were both as tired as a tired person who was tired. They agreed that today would go down in history as one of the most fun days EVER!! They had achieved so much, and so many people had come to see the new sweet shop. What's more, the comments had been universally complimentary.

Granny Bubbles was finally confident that her little business was going to be a success and was glad she hadn't listened to all the Naysayers. Sometimes to gain the top prize of self-confidence, you first must feel extremely uncomfortable. This was the reward for all the worry. She could now relax. They slowly ate their soup in exhausted silence, and both headed half beat and half elated home for a good night's sleep.

Chapter Eleven

Days and Knights

The shop had been running smoothly all spring and the season was now changing into summer. Granny Bubbles had acquired a routine of wholesaler visits, running the shop, organising marketing, accounts and sourcing stock from more exotic locations.

Granny Bubbles had even introduced an American Candy section which was selling very well. The American shelves were crammed with Twinkies, Reese's bars and more Tootsie Rolls than you could shake your stick at. This section brought out a surprising number of residents who were from over the pond. Fabulous Alice thought this was very interesting and always quizzed the customers about where they were from and how they came to live in this sleepy shoe town. Mac from New York, Brad from Nevada, Bruce from Florida. It was fascinating. One lady had been working for American Intelligence while living in the town. It occurred to Fabulous Alice she might not be that great at keeping secrets if she was telling her what she did for a living.

Success seemed to be about keeping stock fresh and finding new and different reasons for people to keep coming back to the shop. The locals were kindly supporting Granny Bubbles venture further by returning, again and again and it was all going very well indeed.

As time rolled on Granny Bubbles tried to figure out a pattern in the trading hours during the daytime. What days and times were the busiest? It appeared unsurprisingly that a large part of the day's income was after school and on Saturdays.

Undeniably anything could happen in the cold light of day at Granny Bubbles Sweet Shop during this time. The girls named rush hour "The Sherbet Stampede" It happened between 3:10 pm until exactly 4:10 pm each day, not a moment sooner or a moment later. The after schoolers were like a stampede of hungry buffalo leaving a trail of bikes propped up without care against the 100-year-old window panes. This was the hour of the day that terrified anybody who worked during this time. It was a solid hour to put your head down and motor on. There was no choice.

Friday treat day was an unwritten rule for most parents on the way back from school, popping in for a treat for the children. This shift was on a whole different level of fear but worse than that Friday Treat Day on the last day of the month on payday was just craziness!! Mere mortals could not work this shift alone. The Sherbet Stampede needed more hands-on deck.

Enter Maia Moo. Granny Bubbles had known Maia Moo her entire life. She was a friend's daughter and was only the third person to have welcomed Maia Moo into the world when she was born. Maia Moo arrived into the world with jet black, feathery, fluffy hair like a fancy silky chicken. Later, surprisingly she had transformed into a blond-haired petit beautiful schoolgirl in her last years of senior school. She had fairy tale long blonde Rapunzel style hair, with big blue sparkly eyes and a perfect white-tooth smile. She was a doll. As sweet as she looked, she was as tough as iron nails and would kill any unkindness with wicked humour and a quick snap of her tongue. Granny Bubbles loved her. She was only 15, and it's true to say that custom had increased tenfold since she started. There seemed to be a trend of 15-year-old schoolboys had suddenly gained a penchant for sweets when she was working and would often wander in with dreamy wishing eyes that Maia Moo would take any notice of them. Which of course she never did. She didn't have any time for

Wally's. She had far too much fun with her girlfriends for that nonsense.

Maia Moo would finish school and run up ahead of all her school mates, ready for her after school first job. Her job was to put jars back into their places on the shelves. It was so busy during the sherbet stampede there was little or no hope of Fabulous Alice keeping up with demand. Sometimes behind the counter, she would be knee-deep in jars. They were piling up for Maia Moo to return them quickly. Maia Moo and Fabulous Alice were a well-oiled machine working together like dancing swans and nailing the sherbet stampede to a tee.

At 3:10 pm, into the shop, would trickle the tiny school children from the primary school. Saint Patrick's

School was just around the corner. These pupils would often bend their parent's ears until they relented for a Raspberry Blue Mega lollipop to dip in a small bag of homemade lemon sherbet on the way home from school. Granny Bubbles made her own bright sunset yellow sherbet with an extra citric acid zing to make your tongue salivate, and your ears itch at the thought of it. It was a top seller.

There was a particular girl who would only 'Need' exactly ten bubble gumballs. BUT. They had to be bright yellow. Every day without fail, she would bound into the shop after school for the gumballs. They were one penny each, and it was far more labour intensive than any other sane business in the land would stand for, tediously counting ten yellow bubble gums out of a jar of a zillion of multi-coloured gums. If business was quiet Maia Moo would pick them out and put them into small bags for the future to save everyone time and effort later. She was a forward thinker you see and was always looking for ways they could improve service. "Work smarter, not harder!" she would exclaim! Wise words for a youth thought Granny Bubbles.

This little dot, and her yellow gum balls, spent a total of fifty pence per week but she was working through 2600 bubble gums a year, which over 52 weeks of the year notched up to £26. It's funny how sales all add up. That little girl soon turned into a bigger girl. She earned more money from a paper round so each day she would spend a bit more. She was now older and wiser so any colour bubble-gum would be fine. She was now paying 30p per day plus a bag of cherry sticks for £1. It meant her daily spend was now £1.30, which would mean an annual spend of over £300 per year. That was nearly half the shop rent for a month! Granny Bubbles had looked after this little girl and every other young customer knowing this is what was what required for successful long-haul business growth. It was always Granny Bubbles Sweet Shop company policy to make sure every customer was welcome. Never to make a fuss of even the smallest transaction because a low sale today could mean a bigger deal tomorrow. If every customer, large or small, were treated well, they would keep coming back for more and guess what, they did.

After the small children had come and gone, then followed the senior school pupils. The seniors came in group herds. They were teaming up with whoever lived on the same road on the way home. The seniors would amuse themselves during the dull walk home with laughs and chops full of sweets. They ascended like trampling Wildebeest on a fresh patch of green grass in the Serengeti. Desperate for their sweet fix.

The local senior school was called "The Knights College". For me and my ridiculous imagination, this conjured up images of a school for Knights. I daydreamed of pocket-sized adolescent would-be-Knights. All dressed in child size chainmail armour with shiny jewelled starter swords buckled into their belts. Imagining each morning, they were heading off to learn about the skills of Knighthood, I chuckled those parents might be loading up their beloved children each morning, with packed lunches and a backpack full of learning books like 'How to Domesticate a Dragon, Defence Education Against Fire Breathing and Attacks and Horsemanship Skills for Jousting'. Would the Mum's on the school run bundle them up with shields and have them wear metal boots? I pondered about schoolings on swordsmanship, cloak cleaning, lance polishing and maintenance, chain mail preservation and helmet care. There really would be a lot to learn about Knighthood now that I thought about it, which was too much thinking and not enough working according to my boss.

Unfortunately, I was utterly wrong. The somewhat less compelling reason it was named The Knights College was far less stimulating. The school was named after Sir Alfred Knight who was a local scholar and an academic. His early innovation for the shoe industry and shoelace services was enough to warrant the naming. I much preferred my story of mini-Knights at a school desk learning.

For a brief hour of the day, you could not see the shop floor for Knights pupils tearing through the sweet shop like a swarm of locusts. STARVING hungry after ditching hot school meals and saving scraps of dinner money to buy their favourite snaffle on the way home.

In the summer months, Granny Bubbles installed a large slush drinks machine and could competitively knock out ice slushed drinks cheaper than anywhere in town. She concocted her own syrup flavours to add to the ice and had a thousand different varieties. Each day would be two different flavours and two different colours such as cola, lime, lemonade, dandelion and burdock. Sometimes she would muddle up the colour creating a blue mango or a green tangerine flavour. She called it "Mystery Monday". People literally couldn't get enough of them. The queue would slip out of the door and down the street, on a hot day for at least a quarter of a mile. If it were too long, Maia Moo would be pouring and selling slush while Fabulous Alice just stayed selling sweets. It was a Slush Stampede.

The regulars were worth the effort. Some were peculiar, some were fun, and some were grumpy. It was a lottery as to who would grace the shop with their presence. You could learn a lot about human nature from this little shop. All walks of life were possible.

In amongst all the chaos, a tiny lad called Ethan James with dark brown curly hair and beautiful olive skin. He was as quiet as a mouse. He stood out to Granny Bubbles because most boys his age were like tornadoes with school bags with absolutely no sense of personal space or awareness. He was different. He wasn't boisterous or reckless but controlled and calm instead. He spent precisely 32p each day on mini pink and white marshmallows. He had twigged on early that the lighter the sweet, the more you could fit in a bag. So, for 32p (which happened to be the change from his mid-morning snack at school for a packet of crisps and a flapjack costing 68p), he could fill an entire paper bag with mini marshmallows and munch on them all the way home. Ethan always left with a smile and seemingly delighted with his own cunning. He loved nothing more than getting as much as he could for his money. To him, every penny counted. He eventually grew up to be VERY good with money. So good in fact that other people gave him their hard-earned cash to invest in companies he thought would make a profit. He worked in the city in London, earning millions as a stockbroker selling and buying shares in other people's businesses. He was so thrifty with money that he eventually saved so much money that he never needed to work again. He bought a house on the beach in the Bahamas in the Caribbean and spent his days teaching tourists to snorkel! He didn't really need to work at all, and he just liked helping people gain a new skill. He enjoyed showing them the sea turtles, stingrays, dolphins, and sharks. While snorkelling an extraordinary sight could often occur. On his beach lived wild pigs that would swim alongside the class in the sea, waiting for titbits of food from the snorkelers. Imagine that! Sea swimming pigs! Granny Bubbles thought that was amazing when he came back as an adult, and she vowed to visit him one day on his beach with a bag of mini marshmallows and maybe fruit for the pigs.

Chapter Twelve

The Baker and Barrister

James Wittering-Mucklemead was a busy high-end criminal law barrister in the city of London. His job was to defend people who paid him to do so in a court of law. It was a tough job morally for most but not for him. And he always said it was not his job to decide if they were guilty, that was what a judge and jury were for.

Often, he had to defend criminals who had made a career out of crime. His job was to find a loophole, seek any angle he could, to protect his paying client. He would twist, unsettle a story of the prosecution or deny allegations without proof until the judge and jury were hooked or bent into to his way of thinking. He had a beautiful way with words and was a superb storyteller. Mucklemead would pour over and over his clients' story hundreds of times to see what angles he could use to defend them. The hours it took him to do this made him very expensive. But career criminals knew the investment was worth it so that they could get back to filling their wallets with dirty money from ill-gotten gains. His reputation was excellent among them.

Some clients had broken the law in one-off crimes too. One such example was a wicked baker who had deliberately laced rat poison in a batch of freshly baked hot cross buns. In the guise of asking his competitor feedback for his new recipe, he sent the carefully boxed samples of death up to his opponents.

Both shops were very busy bakeries, and there was plenty of trade for both in the large bustling village. But for the wicked baker, it was not nearly enough. He needed more money. Much more. Baking was the only thing he was good at, and his whole adult life was the only trade he knew. It is true that his buttery croissants could make a French man skip with joy and a Belgian could melt into his flaky couque suisse. On a Saturday morning the masses queued for his Market Harborough cheesecake. He really was quite talented. But this was never enough. The narcissistic side of the wicked baker NEEDED all the trade for himself for a good reason.

He was head over heels in love and had to make a lot more money if he was to keep his beloved young beautiful wife, Anastasia Olga Blasenkopf.

Anastasia Olga was 6ft 1inches in flat shoes. Which of course she never wore. She basked in towering over people, especially the wicked baker. He was mesmerised with her, it was probably her long blond hair, legs that went on for miles and the bushiest eyebrows. He was utterly devoted to her and catered to her every whim. She was a very spoilt woman and was fiery as his best oven. Anastasia Olga had high demands and exuberant tastes that were to be met come rain or shine if a peaceful life was to be had.

"I vant a fur coat, I am too cold in zis one, and vile you are at it, I need a new car, zis von ist dirty. Make it red and fast, zis iz too slow"

The demands were endless. But whatever Anastasia Olga wanted Anastasia Olga got.

"I vill need a boat zis summer for my friends and me. I'm bored of being on land, I need open spaces, and I need it now." She was so fierce a lioness would probably cower in her presence.

Anastasia Olga had an almighty voice that filled the air with red anger and shouted so loud on occasion it would make a glass shatter. She also had a terrible habit of throwing things too. Mostly in the direction of the wicked baker if she was displeased in any way. He thrived on her unreasonable behaviour and did everything he could to avoid upsetting her. But this came at a cost and her insatiable needs were becoming more and more expensive.

The hot cross buns were devoured by the lovely competitor baker and all his staff too. They did taste good; it was true. But sadly, one by one, they all keeled over and died a quick, painful death. It was a miserable end to their lives. All in the name of greed.

The next day when the bakery had not opened, and suspicion grew. When they were called to investigate, the police found the very sorry sight of all the bodies. Later in court the police presented their proof to the court. The empty, but for the poison crumbs, wicked bakers branded cake box of and the box of rat poison. This is where Mucklemead initiated his chance to defend. They made a slight error which was to allow the wicked baker to literally get away with the multiple murders. Mucklemead highlighted that the evidence shown by the police

" ...was not in securely sealed and dated standard-issue police evidence bags.".

"Furthermore"... he bellowed loud and clear in court. "This evidence could have been planted by anyone and could have come from anywhere your honour." The investigators at the scene had made a tiny but detrimental error in the case. They had not bagged up the evidence in official police sealed evidence bags. With the judge's agreement, this fact made the case collapse. It was an awful shame for the families of the deceased.

And so, the wicked baker was the only baker left in the village. Reluctantly the village used him because his Belgian milk chocolate eclairs with whipped dairy cream really were to die for. He then hoovered up all the business in the community and lived happily ever after. Well for a short time at least. He met his makers in an unfortunate end after his beloved young wife left him for a very much younger tanned pool boy.

He was heartbroken, to say the least and spent a lot of time distracted. Whilst making a fresh batch of hot cross buns his apron string began to tangle in the industrial cake mixer, and he shot inside the giant bowl it and he was whisked to death. He was quite dead and left the village without any bakers at all. Anastasia Olga was delighted she was left all of his property and money.

By nature, Mucklemead was a phenomenally argumentative man. He was a master at twisting the truth. Even as a child, he would run circles around his parents and teachers, convincing them his version of events was correct. He highlighted angles of an argument that could unhinge your opinion that black was white and wrong was right. He was most convincing and what he did for a living suited him handsomely. He was paid very highly for his skills and lived in a large house in the country near to Granny Bubbles Sweet Shop. However, there was one person who could put him right back in his box.

That was Mrs Mucklemead. She was a sturdy old boot and had him wrapped around her finger. Unlike anyone he ever encountered like police, judges, criminals, parents, teachers...he was far more scared of his wife than of anyone. She could see through him like wet tissue paper. Love must have been her superpower.

She was also a barrister, so she knew what he thought before he knew what he had thought! Which meant he just couldn't lie to her.

True to form he found a chink in her armour though. To keep her sweet by literally keeping her sweet. He merely had to use Granny Bubbles homemade Cola Cubes. They were a taste sensation. Perfect squares of cola flavoured hardboiled sweets, dusted with a smattering of sugar coating on the outside—bright red in colour with an addictive, delicate chew in the middle. Once you cracked the outside, a buttery cola chew blasted your tongue and made your ears tickle and jaw ache from the sharp citric flavour. These were not easy for Granny Bubbles to make. They required great skill. She had to make the chewy centre first at a lower temperature and then wrap the harder square hardboiled sweet over the top. It was a tricky process, but the effort was worth it, though. These cola cubes were award-winning. They were just about the only thing Mr Mucklemead could make Mrs Mucklemead smile with. For that reason, he was a brilliant customer at Granny Bubbles Sweet Shop.

When she popped the tangy cube into her mouth and the world stopped. Any cares she had vanished and her whole focus was enjoying THAT moment. She just closed down into a trance until it was finished.

Mr Mucklemead had learnt early on in his marriage, that confectionery was an efficient way of getting his way. She was not a flowers and chocolate kind of woman. Kola Kubes was the currency required.

He later used confectionery as a weapon in all areas of his personal life and later in his career.

He had been working on a case in London at the Old Bailey. It was a bizarre case. Just the way that Mucklemead liked.

A successful violinist had been found dead in a swimming pool that belonged to an equally successful cellist. They both had an incredibly glittering music career in their own right. Both had played for European royalty, celebrity birthdays, international shows, concerts and even royal weddings.

They were both at the peak of their game, but the prized top job was with the Royal International Orchestra of Excellence. R.I.O.E. was the golden handshake of the orchestra world, the pinnacle of a musical career. You had to be exceptionally talented to join, and getting an invitation was as rare as finding unicorn poo.

The two had been massive rivals for a very long time indeed. Not directly in competition with each other within the orchestra, but more of a personal battle was afoot. They had fought for many years over a beautiful harpist who would pit them against each other for fun. She was as bright as a button and buckets of fun. If the truth be told she was more interested in the conductor, who was an equally pretty lady. The more she pitted them against each other, the more intense the rivalry became. The race heated up with the news that she had been invited to play at the R.I.O.E.

One hot summer evening, the malice took a dark turn for the worse when the violinist visited the cellist's home. He sauntered into the back garden, uninvited with the sole aim of gloating about his summons to join the R.I.O.E. In his wisdom this was his first port of call was taunt his nemesis and make it clear he would win the harpists heart FOREVER.

"So, my little chum. I cannot believe that it has taken THIS long to recognise my immense talent and for the RIOE to choose me and not you to further my already magnificent career. It shan't be too long before she recognises that I am the fairer man, and you are a meagre fat stringed, chubby fingered oaf." Gloated the Violinist with a grin as wide as a jester.

The cellist was enraged beyond imagination. The immediate feeling of jealousy boiled up inside him and a red mist appeared in his eyes. He bubbled and raged like a tornado of fury within his gut. He was livid.

He slowly mimed, wide eyed and red faced. "Fat. Fingered. OAF!!!!!!?". And then a roar left his lungs like an injured wild animal scream.

"RaaaaggggҺhhhhhhhhhhhhhhhhhhhhhhhhhh"

He was so angry he reached for the nearest object to him and picked up his beloved cello. With all his might he thrust it up in the air and swung it clean over the violinist head launching him clean into the pool.

If the blow to the head hadn't killed him, then the drowning certainly did. Cool as a cucumber, the cellist turned on his heels without so much of a pang of regret. Panting slowly to catch his breath back.

The violinist's lifeless body stayed there, floating, fully clothed in the pink pool. There he lay, soulless, until the gardener arrived the next day to see the grim discovery. He called the police.

The cellist regretted nothing. As far as he was concerned the world was a much better place without another filthy violinist in it.

Now, unfortunately for Mucklemead, it was up to him to prove the cellist was innocent. There was not a shred of evidence to suggest that he was honest. With a very dead violinist, in HIS pool with claret blood all over his broken cello.

Unless he could convince the jury that it was a freak act of nature and the wind was responsible for lifting 3kg of Bosnian Maple clean off its stand, high enough and in the right direction to snuff out a talented violinist's life. How... would he get this unusual crime squashed.

He certainly had his hands full with this case and perhaps for once had bitten off more than he could chew. But he was not going to be beaten. Fortunately for the cellist, there were no witnesses that could talk. Only a one-legged black labradoodle called Pluto that witnessed the whole sorry episode. He had taken a vow of silence long ago because well, he was a dog and that's what they do in an emergency.

Mucklemead had gone over every detail of the case back to front and inside out. He could not find a loophole for this dreadful man. He had to pull this one right out of the bag. It was his job, so he had to think harder. He was at a dead loss. He was so perplexed he even asked Mrs Mucklemead what she thought.

As he sat explaining to her about the case, she was nodding in the right places but not listening to a word he had said. She was so engrossed in her cola cube she hadn't listened to anything at all. He looked at her with disappointment, expecting her to be useful but gaining nothing.

Then, a bolt of lightning hit his grey matter. If SHE was so engrossed in that cola cube and not listening to a word that he was saying. Maybe he could get the entire judge and a jury to eat cola cubes while the defence was being presented. They would not hear a thing either. It was a genius plan.

The next morning, Mucklemead stood impatiently outside, waiting for Granny Bubbles to open. The moment she did, he marched in with purpose, grinning at his genius.

"Fifteen separate lots of 100-gram bags of your finest Cola Cubes please." He said with a grin on his face. Quite pleased with himself. If he could pull this plan off, he'd be the talk of the court.

Granny Bubbles wondered why he needed such a large quantity of cola cubes and why it was so urgent of a morning. He was clearly in a rush as he tapped his tie impatiently while she hurriedly weighed each bag.

He paid and promptly and hot-footed it out the door in a flash to go and catch his train.

His plan was borderline ridiculous, but then so was his job. He would try every trick in the book to get a win, after all, he had a reputation to protect. Losing cases was not good for business.

He arrived at court and Mucklemead put his plan into action. Sneakily, he handed a bag of sweets to the security guard Jo, with whom he had been childhood friends. Jo was delighted but then realised nothing was for nothing. Mucklemead asked Jo to slip the rest of the black and white stripy bags in the jury benches and again on the judge's seat before they all arrived. Jo would do anything for a bag of sweets.

Mucklemead changed into his legal wear. That consisted of a black gown with arm slits covered his shoulders down to his ankles, a bright white shirt with two long bands at the front of his collar and pinstriped trousers.

Barrister's heads are historically topped with a peculiar short curled legal wig's that are all handmade from horse's hair. At the back of the wig's, they have two small, curled tails either side. In England, wigs have always been worn in criminal courts to show who is a barrister and who is the judge.

Then it was show time. First, the jury entered their seats slowly. Then the judge entered and started proceedings. "Is the defendant ready for your trial?" asked the court clerk. “I am,” said the Cellist.

The jury was then selected, and the defendant swore on the bible to “tell the truth, the whole truth and nothing but the truth.”

"Very well, proceed" said the judge looking down, baffled at the black and white stripy bag on his bench.

As the prosecution barrister for the family of the murdered violinist, read through his account of the murder, the stripy bags began to rustle, and “umm's and ahhhs” could be heard coming from the jury area. The hardboiled square boxes of heaven were clattering around in the judge and jury's mouths, and they could not hear a thing. It was working! The whole panel was so enjoying the delicious cola cubes that they were away with the fairies. They hadn't listened to a single word the prosecution had said. It was all just a fuzzle of noise in the background. The prosecution’s case was long enough that the whole bag of cola cubes could be consumed in one go. Not a single cola cube was left. Crumpled black and white stripy bags were scattered everywhere. Even the judge had lost track of proceedings after noshing his way through the delicious, Moorish, squares of cola delight.

"... and to that, your honour, members of the jury, is why we think the defendant is guilty of murder in the second degree with intent to cause serious injury that unfortunately resulted in death." finished the prosecution.

The jury silently looked at each other in horror. Not even the judge acknowledged his gluttonous mistake, and that *he* should have known better.

In the courtroom was a buzz of sugar fuelled people. They were itching to get this over with and get on with their day.

Now it was Mucklemead's time to shine.

"...he has suggested it was nothing more than the wind that had lifted the giant cello, hit the unfortunate deceased violinist and knocked him clean into the pool."

The plan had worked a treat. The jury had not listened to a word that the prosecution had presented. Technically there was not a lot of hard evidence that they could hear to convince them of a murder. But that was because they physically couldn’t hear over the cola cube crunching going on in their own mouth.

The judge and the jury all agreed it was an act of Mother Nature and declared the cellist free as a bird.

Mucklemead could not believe his luck. He had an unbelievably high rate of accomplishment getting criminals off the hook and this case was another sting in his violin bow.

Business just got busier and busier. So did Granny Bubbles for that matter. Mucklemead was her most top-grossing customer. She hadn't realised for a moment she was an accessory to his questionable practices but still, it paid the bills.

Chapter Thirteen

The Little Shrew

"Good morning me 'duck!" Mr White typically entered the shop with a quick spring in his tall step, and always with a friendly smile. "Quarter of your finest sugar-free pineapple cubes and a quarter of sugar-free barley twists please me 'duck!". Like many, he seemed pleased to be there, dashing in and dashing out. They seldom had any further conversation than the basic greetings, order and a fair well.

"Me 'duck" was a wonderful greeting within Northamptonshire that most people of a certain age used. It is a term of endearment and generally used in place of a person's name. Nobody knows where it came from or why people greet each other as ducks. But it is quite charming and jolly, so why not?

Mr White was a true gentleman. Opening doors for ladies, tipping his head for fellow gents and beaming with manners to all he met.

His head topped with sparse, wispy white hair that was as groomed as it could be. Kind big brown eyes framed by his silver spectacles. He wore a very distinctive, heavy leather jacket. It was edged with a thick brown woolly sheepskin collar and buckles that swung down at the sides. The cuffs sported zips halfway up the arms and had sheepskin edges too.

Ever since the shop had opened, he always sported a dependable, compact wardrobe that consisted of black trousers, a checked shirt with smart brown Northamptonshire made 'Loakes' shoes, which could have been 40 or 50 years old that still looked brand new. Northamptonshire is famous for magnificent quality men's leather shoes that last decades. His uniform, comfortingly, did not ever change.

It was a brief exchange and a finely tuned routine. It used to be pineapple cubes and barley sugar but later changed. "Quarter of sugar-free pineapple cubes and a quarter of sugar-free barley twists please me 'duck!"

Then one sunny day he came in without his leather jacket. It was a bit of a shocker to see him wearing a black suit, a white collared shirt with a long black tie. Whilst he looked smart, Mr White looked much less chipper than usual. He looked gloomy and pale and exhausted. Granny Bubbles had automatically headed straight to the sugar-free section when she seen him walking past the window, but Mr White stopped her in her tracks. "Ohhhh me ‘duck, not today. I have a different request. Today me ‘duck, I would like a quarter of raspberry ruffles, and a quarter of white toffee bonbons please me duck."

She found herself entirely in the wrong part of the shop. She looked up at him to see his grey, tired face. Quickly she relocated to the bon bon section and picked up the full jar of dusty white bon bons that puffed out a cloud of dust as she opened the jar. On her way back to the scales she plucked the raspberry ruffles jar from the chocolate section and began to weigh out his order.

"Did you fancy a change from sugar-free?" she enquired gingerly. But really, she knew about black ties and the reason people wore them. She knew the mourning wear all too well.

"No me duck, I shen't be buying those anymore. No need. The sugar-free sweets were for my wife. But unfortunately, my dear Muriel has now passed away. Evil cancer got the ol' girl in the end. This morning was her funeral, where we said goodbye for the last time. It has been a long old journey, but it has all come to an end now, and finally, my Mu is pain-free and at peace."

Granny Bubbles shook her head softly and dipped her head in sorrow. "I hate Cancer" she said. "It steals all the good ones. At least, as you say, she is at peace and without pain. It must have been awful for you both?"

"Yes gal, been painful to watch and more painful to let her go." Granny Bubbles continued bagging his sweetie order and delicately handed them over to him. As she did, she grasped his hand to comfort him looking him dead in the eye. "I am so sorry" She whispered.

He took a deep breath in and was about to turn away but then said. "I know it seems odd to come to a sweet shop on the day of Air Mu's funeral, but your shop always makes me feel better. The smell of the sugar is an escape…just for a moment anyway. I thought I would come in for some sweets for the grandkids. They're coming by after school to see me. Lovely little things they are too."

Granny Bubbles handed him his change.

"It was the one time in the week that I got a little rest from Air Mu's illness, I looked after her every moment of the day and night " He bravely expelled.

Granny Bubbles was very sad for him. She knew just what it was like to lose a spouse. Even though she didn't like her husband, she sometimes missed the idea of having him about. But to lose someone you truly loved must have been heart breaking.

"We knew, me ‘duck, she wasn't going to live forever, she had been very poorly with the cancer, but you and your shop played a big role in soothing her each week! I must at least thank YOU for that.” He mustered a smile.

“One medication for cancer is called chemotherapy, it makes people lose their appetite, and the taste buds suffer too. So poor Muriel couldn’t even have the enjoyment of food anymore. The only thing she could taste and enjoy were your tangy sugar-free pineapple cube sweets. It was the one moment she could snatch a little pleasure, and I shall be forever grateful to you for stocking them for us.” Recalled Mr White.

“After everything that she had survived throughout her life, it's nothing short of cruel that cancer would snatch her from me." He continued.

Granny Bubbles felt her heart break for him. Mr White looked very washed away and it was a wonder he was still standing. It occurred to her he could probably do with a sit-down. It was her break time, and she wondered if he would like to join her for a cup of tea out the back.

“Mr White, can I make you a cup of tea before you head home. So that you can gather a bit of strength?” He took a deep breath in and nodded a yes. He was grateful and took Granny Bubbles up on her kind offer. "Yes, me ‘duck, I should appreciate a hot cuppa tea very much.” He smiled at her kindness.

Granny Bubbles led him through to the rainbow ribbon curtain out to the back, where they both sat on the stools, sipping hot tea. "I can tell you a few things about my Mu that would make your toes curl. She was no ordinary woman you see." Mr White bravely began to relay Muriel's life story to Granny Bubbles.

All this time, Mr White had frequented the shop, and this was the first time they had spoken at length about her. Generally, he was on the move to get back to her. He didn't like to be away from her for too long you see.

Muriel White had been a fascinating young lady in her early adulthood. Granny Bubbles was more than a little surprised to learn she had been a secret agent during the second world war for the British. She was a massive help during the French resistance movement, when fighting the Germans fiercely from occupying France. It was a bitter battle, and her role was pivotal in the fight to keep France French!

Muriel's family were wealthy landowners back in Australia and farmed thousands and thousands of acres with cattle, but their primary income was leasing their land for gold mining and receiving a cut of everything mined. Muriel's father was a clever man who knew a good way to earn a buck or two.

In her early teens, Muriel was sent to a fancy school in Northamptonshire as a boarding student. Education was paramount to her success; it was there she learnt several languages, etiquette and customs.

But for three other very bright, wealthy girls, the school was predominantly boys. It was unusual for girls to attend prestigious schools, let alone board. But her father paid handsomely for the placement of his only daughter. Muriel schooled with many European children too and loved learning their diverse ways of life. She had many boys as friends too and charmed them all with a view that she could stay with their families all over Europe during holidays and only went back home to Australia at Christmas if she had too. The families adored her and treated her like family.

Her family had a second homes in London, Paris and Austria for skiing so she would see them there too when they were over, if she wasn't too busy in Florence or Amsterdam. Europe was Muriel's playground!

Her life was all about adventure and she had a whale of a time learning about and meeting as many people as she humanly could along the way. Muriel thrived in her English school. She even adored the grey drizzly weather. England felt like home.

Muriel was a clever girl emotionally and academically at school, and she use oozed charisma on the teachers and was a master at persuasion. Quite an anomaly for her age. Her father was just the same, hence his success in an all but barren land. She had an air of confidence and was excellent at communicating her needs to anyone who would listen. Her leadership, even at an early age, was evident. She was head girl, hockey coach, captain of cricket for the boys and was the choirmaster too. She wasn't bossy, but she was great at getting the best out of people and had an intense winning streak. Her encouragement of others really got the best out of them. She had an angelic face to boot, and butter probably wouldn't melt in her mouth because she was so calm and relaxed. Muriel was as far away from what you thought a spy should look like, as could be and THAT was her superpower. Angel faced with the cunning of a fox and the persuasion skills of a puppy!

Muriel considered England her home and after school she stayed in London doing very little that didn’t involve partying with other rich folk. When the war broke out, as an Australian citizen, it left her in a bit of a quandary and she so wanted to be useful, but Muriel initially was refused a position in the armed forces.

She decided to go to France on her own steam and find a way to help. She desperately wanted to be involved and considered herself an asset and knew her skills in language, persuasion and deception would come in handy somewhere.

She stayed with an old school friend's family in France initially. Now fluent in French. Soon she rented a small shop which she turned into a small grocery shop. It wasn't long before her the war engaged her talents. Setting to task almost immediately two British RAF pilots had been shot down out of the sky by the Germans sea defences and amazingly, they managed to parachute into a forest just outside the walled city of Rouen.

Luckily a French mushroom picker found them and not a German. She helped bury the parachutes and laid the men under hessian sacks on her donkey and cart and took them straight to the grocers where she knew the Australian might help. Muriel settled them into the cellar with good food and beds.

If the Germans caught them, they would have been killed. But also, if the Germans found out what Muriel had been up too, the Germans would have killed her too. But she didn't care. She had an inherent dislike for Germans after a school colleague had perished in their hands.

Muriel would feed them to help build up strength and send them on to the next safe house armed with clothing, food and money.

Every time an ally was found alive and needed protection, they were sent to Muriel.

Soon she set up an extensive network, persuading fellow French resistance owners with cafes and wine bars and shops as safe places to get them out to neutral Spain so that they could get to safety and carry on the fight.

It was a dangerous journey for them, but the alternative was death, and Muriel was brave, calculating determined and sly. Muriel's System, as it was known, managed to assist a good few hundred allies to get to Spain, but before long the Germans caught on to her.

It was time for Muriel to use her own system and make her way to Spain for safety because the Germans put a bounty on her head, which meant if someone caught her and brought her to the Germans dead or alive, they would receive a handsome bag of cash. There were a lot of people looking for money in those days, so it was no longer safe to be Muriel.

Travelling hundreds of miles through Frances's hot, dangerous German invaded territory was a nerve-racking time. She had eaten very little for weeks, had been shot at more than once, chased and on one occasion even captured. She was taken to prison but soon escaped that effort. The more difficult it became the braver she got.

Throughout her journey, she kept herself as neat as possible and always wore bright red lipstick with immaculate curled hair. Just because there was a war on did not mean her appearance should suffer. She looked too glamourous to be a prisoner of war and persuaded the guard in her best German accent that she was the staff who had accidentally been locked in. It worked a treat. Muriel had mastered many European accents from her time spent with her school friends. On the farm back in Australia, she had learned to shoot at Dingo's trying to kill her father's cattle. So, Muriel was a crack shot with any gun. She always carried a small silver gun in her pocket and was never afraid to use it!

Eventually she made it to Spain, where for at least a little while she could relax. It was a dangerous existence, but the thrill of outwitting the Germans was a reward in itself for her.

She made it back to the UK, coloured her hair blonde, added glasses and a mass of fresh red lipstick.

Now, this indeed meant war! As soon as she could, she would go back to continue to help. Word got back to the English military chiefs of her bravery, proficient organisation skills and determination to assist in the war effort and they called her up with an extraordinary mission. They asked her to head a group of like-minded ladies as female spies to which she agreed immediately.

After a stint of basic military training, the military issued her with a vast amount of money, for bribery and firearms for defence, which she kept in a beautiful leather briefcase.

The girls flew back to France and parachuted into Rouen Forest, where a mushroom cart awaited to continue her work. Their mission was to sabotage German plans and infiltrate their offices to steal important documents. On one mission she was pretending to be a German cleaner and boldly skipped off with many important secret documents hidden in her dirty mop bucket with a secret compartment under the bucket. It looked just like a full bucket, but when you lifted a top bucket out there was room inside underneath for stashing items. These documents had plans and times of attacks against the British. That meant the Allies could be well-armed and attack first at the correct locations and more importantly, at the right time. It's thought she saved millions of lives by scuppering the Germans plans. All while assuming the identity of a German cleaner.

The enemy finally realised somebody was stealing information from the inside but could never quite pin it down to her. She quit while she was ahead and bolted off before being caught.

She evaded capture so many times they named her 'The Little Shrew'. Invisible and fast. The Little Shrew again had a bounty on her head. They once caught her, and frog marched her in for questioning. Even then, she persuaded the prison guard she was again lost, and he miraculously let her go! She couldn't believe her luck.

Muriel thrived on the excitement and was almost a little disappointed when the war ended.

After the war, several countries decorated Muriel with many medals from the allied forces. Australia, France, UK and even America. She vowed to leave her adventurous streak behind and quit while she was ahead, settle down to be a normal lady and hopefully live happily ever after.

Mr White had been a Royal Air Force spitfire pilot in his day. He attended basic training at the age of 20 to become a pilot and was soon off to fight. Early on in his career, his plane was shot down by German sea defences and he parachuted into a field where he was lucky enough to be found by a mushroom picker and was sent to a helpful Australian lady who could guide him to safety. Of course, he was one of the first pilots Muriel had helped get to Spain. After the war they met by chance at a tea dance.... and the rest was history.

"And that is how I met my Mu." Said Mr White What a story thought Granny Bubbles. She was flabbergasted.

From that day Granny Bubbles stopped to have a cup of tea with Mr White each week. They became firm friends. He continued to come in for toffee bonbons and raspberry ruffles for his grandchildren.

Each week he would tell her different war stories. He explained why his brown leather pilot's jacket was so important to him. He felt safe and proud to wear it. He was wearing it when he was shot out of the sky, and kept it hidden in a sack all the way home on his awful journey through France to Spain. It kept him warm on icy nights and he felt strong and invisible in it. After that, he wore it on every mission for luck.

When his career as a pilot finished, he still wore it. It was his identity, his comfort and his pride. Only good things happened in that brown leather jacket, and he didn't care who knew it.

When Mr and Mrs White had enough excitement for one lifetime, they retired to concentrate on their joint hobby. Throughout their 40-year marriage they collected war memorabilia. Once she had sadly passed away, it was time to find new homes for the war memorabilia that they had amassed over the years. It just seemed too painful to see at home without Mu to enjoy it.

Remarkably a London Museum had offered to buy the entire collection for a staggering £1.2 million. Mr White was gobsmacked. They were never poor and lived beautifully on Muriel's fathers' inheritance so all of the £1.2 million was donated to Royal British Legion which supports lifelong help to servicemen and woman and their families. He kept a little for himself to buy a vintage bicycle that was used at Bletchley Park for zipping code-cracking information around the site. It was in a terrible state, but he vowed to bring it back to life as his pet project.

Mr White kept to his routine of popping down the High Street each week to buy his grandson and granddaughter one hundred grams of Raspberry ruffles and one hundred grams of toffee bonbons in his heroic leather jacket. He was one of Granny Bubbles favourite customers, and she looked forward to seeing Mr White each week and they became firm friends.

Chapter Fourteen

Wine Gums and Rock

Tuesday morning at 9:01 am was always the same. He was ALWAYS the first to arrive through the door. Mr Henry Lack would wait for the shop door to be opened for him. He had two walking sticks and would tap on the door, with one of them holding himself up carefully with the other. This was his signal to open the door.

The first time Mr Lack had ever visited the shop was quite a memorable one. Granny Bubbles had opened up on her own that day because Fabulous Alice was in late. She was sitting a school maths exam that she had been worried about for some time, so had taken the morning off to revise.

In Mr Lack had wandered. The door had already been propped open, in anticipation of the postman delivering some heavy boxes full of jawbreakers. Granny Bubbles looked him in the eyes and smiled at him as she always did and greeted him. He replied "Hello!" quietly standing frozen in awe of all the colourful jars.

It was the standard behaviour of any human who had entered the shop. It generally took some time for the delights to sink in. The smell of every British confection in one place was breath-taking. The colours were an assault on the eyes.

He propped himself up against the giant candy pole in the middle of the shop and just stared for what seemed like ages. As his eyes wandered around the shop slowly sucking the experience all in, Granny Bubbles explained to him in some length where everything was and what categories were where. She explained that the Liquorice all sorts were in the liquorice section; the chews were over here, and the mints were over there. The man had his back turned to her the entire time.

After he had sucked in all the free confectionery aromas, he turned to Granny Bubbles. He smiled. She smiled back. He smiled, so she smiled back. So, he smiled again. As lovely as this was, these smiles were not going to pay the bills.

"Is there anything I can get you?" she asked, breaking the silence.

He looked at her and smiled, and with his stick, he pointed his stick to the Liquorice all sorts.

She grabbed the pot. "How much would you like?" She asked.

But Henry Lack was facing away and didn't acknowledge her at all. It was like she was invisible. She patted herself to make sure she was indeed still there, and she hadn't vanished. It was not being lost on her that this was an unusual encounter, as folk were generally quite keen to talk about sweets. She was pretty patient with people, but this chap seemed to be bordering on rude. She raised her voice a little higher and louder again.

"HOW MUCH WOULD YOU LIKE?"

She was holding the jar poised and ready to pour into the weighing pan scales. This sale was getting harder by the minute.

He turned to face her and held his hand out with £2 in change.

"£2 worth?"

She asked. Henry Lack nodded with enthusiasm and a wide smile. He had a lovely smile in fact and had such a friendly face. It was fair to say Mr Lack was a handsome chap. He was very tall and well built. He had neatly trimmed full grey head of hair, funky spectacles and a pristine ironed short-sleeved pink shirt. His appearance was clearly important to him. They exchanged cash and sweets, and he turned around to walk away.

He reached the door but then stopped short and whispered to her

"Lime Guns "

Granny Bubbles had bent down to pick up some Aniseed Balls that had escaped. When she popped back up, he was staring at her. While she was down there, she had not realised he had spoken to her. Granny Bubbles was now wondering why he was staring at her in silence. It was turning into a most peculiar interaction. She smiled. He smiled. She smiled, and then he finally whispered “?"

"Wine Hums?" She enquired

"Wine Guns?" he repeated a little slower and louder.

She was clueless and left scratching her hair bun. Out of the corner of her eye, she spied the WINE GUMS. She swiftly pulled the jar off the shelf and presented it like a sommelier would offer a fine wine in a classy restaurant.

His face lit up. "Wine Huns !!!" He immediately pulled a £2 coin out of his pocket and held it out. Granny Bubbles weighed them out and handed the paper bag to him. He didn't have a shopping bag, and she realised that with his two walking sticks, he might struggle to multitask, so popped them in a plastic bag so he could bob them over his walking stick handles. As she did, he looked up and mouthed in a whisper

"I am deaf my dear. I can't hear a thing, and this hearing aid is out of battery" he smiled.

"I can lip read though," he told her.

Well, this explained everything. Granny Bubbles then realised she had been talking to him in great length and he hadn't heard a word she'd said! Each time she had spoken, his back was facing her so he couldn't read her lips.

"I have to see your face and your lips then I can read what you are saying to me!" He suggested.

Granny Bubbles smiled and confirmed she understood with a big thumbs up. He put his hand under his chin flat, then pushed it outwards and signed

"Thank you".

Granny Bubbles was delighted she could finally understand. She mirrored his sign language and replied

"Thank you" back.

The next time he came in, she made sure she greeted him with the sign language for "Hello" which is a wave in front of your face. Not dissimilar to a normal hello wave. He was thrilled she had learned it for him. She made sure she was facing him each time she spoke and taught the girls to do the same. From then on, they communicated flawlessly.

They had lengthy chats about all sorts of things. It turned out Mr Lack was a Pastry Chef in London for very fancy restaurants and had a great admiration for all things confectionery. He would bring Granny Bubbles Victorian chocolate moulds which were so detailed and pretty it would wow you to your boots.

He recalled stories of famous people he had made desserts for. Princesses, Prime Ministers, Kings of Pop and many of the world's most celebrities and politicians. His specialities were rum baba’s, macarons, peach eclairs as well as vanilla and strawberry white chocolate pyramid mousse.

He had won awards and had even been a personal pastry chef to a famous rock star. He had gone on tour for many years touring the world and listening to thunderous rock music in the 1970's. So loud that in late life it had caused his hearing to deteriorate. He had no regrets, though. He'd had a professional life full of celebrity and puddings. A life of salted caramel roulade and rock music. What more could you want?

He enjoyed his quiet life and hadn't made any pastry dishes for years. But when he entered Granny Bubbles Sweet Shop, the smell of sugar always brought back fun memories. He always left smiling.

They swapped recipes, and he would always try Granny Bubbles new fudge concoctions and give his professional opinion. He was never convinced to buy any; he was a creature of habit. It was still Liquorice all sorts and Wine Gums. £2 of each. In a bag. Popped on his walking stick handles. He set off down the High Street to get his newspapers and daily goods as he did every Tuesday from then on. He was an excellent customer.

Chapter Fifteen

Marigolds and Murder

The shop door flung open and remained wedged open with a fluorescent pink newspaper bag and trolly. Each Saturday the paper girl called in for her weekly indulgence of Aniseed Balls.

Holly Elizabeth (or Holly Bet as her family called her) was the hardest working paper girl in the town. Each morning before school, she delivered daily newspapers to the masses, every evening she delivered the Kettering Evening Telegraph and on Sundays, her busiest day, she delivered the big fat heavily supplemented Sunday newspapers. Rammed full of magazines and flyers selling creative solutions for arthritis and gardening kneeling pads.

She was a tiny girl with the work ethic of an army general and the strength of a dung beetle. (A dung beetle if you didn't know, can pull kangaroo poo balls 1150 times its own body weight which is the equivalent of a human pulling six full double decker busses, so that's a very strong creature indeed).

Holly Bet was determined to earn as much money as she possibly could. When she was not delivering newspapers, she walked dogs for busy people and babysat for sociable grownups in the evening. Holly Bet was a girl on a mission.

Holly Bet's Grampy was a Lancaster bomber pilot during the war, and they talked a lot about his time flying. She would listen intently to his brave fighting stories, dodging gunfire, bombing targets and taking down enemy German fighter planes that were hell bent on ending his life. Tales of determination to accomplish his missions and stay alive to tell the tale. Which of course he thankfully did.

He would recall to Holly Bet when his fellow pilots that were not so lucky. Tragic tales of capture, gunshot, bombings and prison. Which for him, always made the flight home afterwards taste sweeter, the tranquillity of returning to Blighty in peace. Soaring away from the devastation below. His relief at flying home knowing he would return to his beloved fiancé, alive for another day. It was tough times.

Holly Bet was hooked on his stories. She lapped them all up, eyes wide open and sucking it all up like a sponge. She treasured his exciting tales of bravery and hung on every word of his peacetime flying tales too. He described the tranquillity of being high up and away from the rat race with only the purring engine noise for company. Darting through the fluffy white clouds and seeing endless blue sky ahead. It was always clear and sunny above the clouds. Guaranteed to make you feel happy.

On her paper rounds, during soggy grey days, she imagined herself soaring up above the land, looking down at fields, clouds and roads. Watching tiny humans going about their business. Holly Bet longed to fly amongst the geese and red kites. The freedom and the view were all that she could think of morning, noon and night.

For her 14th Birthday Holly Bet's Grampy had bought her one single junior flying lesson and right then, she was just hooked forever. By the end of the hour lesson, she had taken control of the small light aircraft and was Controlling the plane herself. She learned the basics of taking off and landing. But the real reward was flying. It was a crystal-clear day, and she could see the yellow rapeseed and green wheat fields as far as the eye could see. All framed in clear blue sky with a slight curve of the edge of earth. The view was magical. Just like Grampy had described. It was such a thrill and one she decided she would never EVER go through her life without. Come rain or shine, she HAD to find a way to do this again.

Unfortunately, her passion was rather expensive, but she needed to fund it somehow. Her parents were comfortable, but like most families they lived month to month. As much as they would have liked to fund her flying, it just was not to be. But they did what they could.

She calculated that she could just about afford single lessons if she saved all of her money JUST for her lessons. It would cost a full month just to pay for an hour in the sky. It was VERY expensive. Such was her determination, that she took on extra rounds and walked dogs as much as she could. She worked so hard any time spare that she had away from school and birthdays and Christmas, she always requested money towards lessons. It was all she lived for. The buzz of the next lesson.

Granny Bubbles sweet shop was the *only* treat Holly Bet allowed herself once a week. £1.50 worth of shiny burgundy spheres of aniseed joy. Holly truly appreciated every ball. She worked very hard, but nevertheless the effort was worth it, she truly loved flying so much she would sacrifice her time and money for the love of it. Each month she kept Granny Bubbles up to date on her flying lessons and all she had learnt.

At least Holly Bet's paper rounds were anything but boring. She bounced out of bed early each morning, wide awake and ready for paper round adventures ahead. Nearly every week something interesting would occur. Probably because she was one of the first to be up and out in the morning. First to see any situations that had happened in the middle of the night that were nearly always discovered first by Holly Bet.

Sometimes she had random helping hands in her quest to fly. One Sunday morning whilst ramming a big fat News of the World in Mr Freemans letterbox. Holly Bet was astonished to have stumbled upon hundreds of £10 notes littered everywhere on his front lawn. It was an odd sight as you can imagine. She rubbed her eyes frantically and pinched her hand to see if she was dreaming. Hundreds of dew-covered notes, soggy and glistening in the sun. The queens' head twinkling in the sun's rays. She paused, not knowing whether to seize the opportunity to frantically stuff the cash in her paper bag and plead ignorance? After all, those flying lessons wouldn't pay for themselves! Or should she be honest, knock on the door and let Mr Freeman know about the bizarre sight. Holly Bet was an honest girl and a lie like that would burn her insides, so she honourably elected the later.

She gently rang the doorbell only once. Still unsure of what the correct etiquette was to wake someone from their slumber, to advise them of a bizarre situation. He poked his head out of the open bedroom window from upstairs. Peering down, annoyed and sleepy eyed to see all the soggy cash about his lawn. He froze. And then gasped. Closing the window and racing down the stairs outside. He realized immediately what he had done. "Help me quickly before Mrs Freeman sees. I will be in very deep trouble if she gets wind of this."

Holly obliged and helped a panicked Mr Freeman scrape up all the money.

"She'll go blooming mad!" he chuntered.

After they had gathered it all up Mr Freeman, sweating like a racehorse, explained to Holly Bet how the soggy money had arrived in his front garden.

It turned out Mrs Lois Freeman had delightfully had a big win at bingo the night before. She had placed the money on her bedside table to take to the bank as soon as they were open again. Mr Freeman had also had a great night the night before at the Cat and Carrot pub. It is safe to say he had a few too many red wines and had not really been in charge of all of his faculties.

Mr and Mrs Freeman had a volatile relationship and spent the best part of it trying to outdo one another in making the other's life as difficult as possible. Lois had refused to cook for him that night after he was exceptionally rude to her during the day when he called her a "Poisonous Elf". 'You reap what you sew' in her mind, and she was not prepared to go out of her way to accommodate him.

On his return from The Cat and Carrot, he stumbled all the way home, ravenous with hunger and sozzled to the core. She was of course fast asleep.

Bumbling around in the kitchen, he opened the oven door and was horrified to find it completely empty. No dinner. Not a morsel. Just an empty plate with a post-it note.

"Enjoy your dinner, oh no you can't because I didn't make you any!

With Love, The Poisonous Elf"

He was ever so cross. With his red wine induced bravery, he marched upstairs. Scanned the bedroom as best he could see and found her all tucked up and snoring soundly. He spied her bedside cabinet and found her bingo winnings. Out of pure spite, he locked onto the lot and threw them all clean out of the bedroom window like confetti at a wedding. Closing the window, he promptly and proudly took himself off to the spare bedroom and slept soundly until Holly Bet knocked on the door to save his bacon.

In the cold light of day, without his red wine shield, he knew just how much trouble he would be in with the "Poisonous Elf".

Luckily for him it was Holly Bet who found all the cash and not a scallywag who might just have skipped off and pocketed it all. It was still very early, and the sun was just peeping over the horizon. The longer they scooped it up the more the memories were coming back to him.

"Take that old hag!" he recalled saying as he thew the bundles of cash out of the window. "Not making me any dinner...I'll show you, miserable faced sow."

After they gathered up the cash, bundled it up and made the garden good again. Mrs Freeman was none the wiser of his drunken rants and knew nothing of how close she came to losing her winnings. She was a little bemused as to why the money was soggy. Blaming herself for spilling her bedside water over it. It seemed he had just about gotten away with it this time.

Mr Freeman was so grateful that Holly Bet had saved his bacon. He gave her five, dry £10 notes out of his wallet, Holly Bet was delighted. Of course, the £50 went straight into her savings tin for flying lessons.

The very next week, on her early morning adventure's she found a doctor's bag. The week after that a mislaid purse. She found lost cats, missing dogs and even a wandering lone tortoise. Every day there was something new and every time she was rewarded in cash for her help. It was remarkable how much it all kept adding up.

Early one Saturday morning towards the end of her paper round. Holly Bet had delivered a ridiculously large Saturday Times to Mr Potters huge house as she wandered up the garden path, not a blade of grass was out of place. It had been known he could often be seen sieving his gravel, sifting out unsightly large stones to ensure they were all uniform. Perpetually pulling tiny weeds out of his stone wall. His life was impeccable or so people thought. He was a church going gentleman, pristine in appearance and immaculate in every way possible. He was, it had to be said, a pillar of the community. Always litter picking, organising coffee mornings and fundraising for the village school.

Holly Bet reached the large white post box on the outside of his beautiful home. Something stopped her dead in her tracks. Out of the corner of her eye she caught a very grim sight that made the hairs on the back of her neck stand on end. A small grey pointy finger with barbie pink nail polish sprouting up through the marigold flower bed, pointing directly at the house. Holly Bet had to rub her eyes in disbelief and compute what exactly she could see. She slowly and calmy delivered The Times and finishing the next-door neighbours Daily Mail newspaper and ran home to ring Grampy immediately. Grampy and Holly took a drive by to double check the situation and sure enough. There again was the pointy finger. Stiff and still pointing to Mr Potter.

Holly had stumbled upon a murder scene. Grampy and Holly called the police, and a crime scene was erected outside Mr Potters Wisteria clad, immaculate house.

Mr Potter had indeed snuffed out his housekeeper's life and into an early grave. Her crime? She had used a milk pan for boiling breakfast eggs. Apparently, this sent Mr Potter orbital with rage, and he struck his poor housekeeper with the said milk pan over the head as a punishment. Mr Potter could not abide anything that was not adhered to in the correct manner and that included using the correct utensils and cooking equipment. In his mind he was well within his rights to lash out at the heinous crime, and he kept quiet about the housekeeper's death. He buried her in the flower beds in the dead of night and carried on as usual, making sure his garden and his own appearance were immaculate.

That was until Grampy, and Holly called the police and put him in prison where he belonged until the end of time. The poor housekeeper was laid to rest properly by her family and friends. Marigolds were NOT allowed at the funeral.

Holly filled Granny Bubbles in on all of her adventures. Each week when she came in for her Aniseed Balls. Granny Bubbles wondered if she sometimes made these stories up until later, sure enough, Holly would be front page of The Evening Telegraph that she delivered herself.

"Paper Girl Hero Snares Village Murderer".

Holly was awarded a big fat Crimestoppers cash reward. Of course, this went straight towards her flying lessons. She was soaring above them clouds in next to no time after that!

Chapter Sixteen

Fry's Peppermint Cream Heist

She was a very unlikely thief, but really what does a thief really look like? Very few people can honestly put their hand on their heart and say they have never stolen a thing? So, thieves come in all shapes and sizes.

Even Granny Bubbles was not as pure as the freshly fallen snow. In fact, Mr Swan would have been horrified had he known each time he had turned his back to weigh out her beloved bubble gums, the angelic and innocent-looking Violet Rose had sneaked a jelly cherry in her chops from the open box next to the till. She was so good at pilfering and had pinched them so many times that she had precisely timed eating the stolen goodies as fast as she could to the millisecond. She could finish sloshing around the chewy cherry delight only just in time, with seconds to spare before Mr Swan would turn around to hand over her wares. It gave Violet Rose a bit of a buzz. But guilt generally got the better of her before she left the shop. To balance out her monstrous crime, she would always try and do a good deed to make herself feel better. If there was any litter outside, she would pop it in the bin. Or maybe the pavement sign outside may have fallen over in the wind, and she would pick it up. Of course, Mr Swan had only ever seen the good deeds, so he thought Violet Rose was very accommodating. She didn't see it as robbing but more sneaking. But in the eyes of the law, stealing is stealing. So, don't pinch sweets!

To be a sweet shop keeper, you had to have eyes in the back of your head. Granny Bubbles had precisely that. Having grown up with two deviant brothers and given birth to a batch of her own reprobates, who regularly tried to pull the wool over her eyes. She was a finely tuned mischief detector and as the saying goes 'You can't kid a kidder'.

Fabulous Alice was on duty the first time the old lady had entered the sweet shop. The old lady was a lovely looking thing. Petit slightly bent over and sporting a beige overcoat and grandma shoes that a mature lady would wear. Lord knows where they buy them, you would never see in any shops. She wore an elegant silk printed pink headscarf over her short silver hair, still in curlers. She slowly pulled a burgundy shopping trolley at sloth speed behind her. She looked rather like a zillion other old ladies on the High Street. At any stage in the day, you could spy hundreds of them like a mass Nanna clone army all bustling away to get back in the warm for tea and knitting.

It was Thursday, fresh new stock delivery day. Fabulous Alice had just that moment opened a brand-new box of Fry's Peppermint Cream Bars. There were forty-eight in a box, and they all sat neatly in a row all facing the correct direction, words towards the customer. She placed them neatly right next to the full box of Fry's Orange Cream Bars and the Fry's Chocolate Cream Bars. Fry’s Chocolate Creams have been around since 1866. They looked very inviting, indeed. If she had one pound for every time a customer asked about the Fry's Mixed Cream Bars, she could have been a multi-millionaire. She could have sailed around the world on an elegant yacht drinking champagne.

It is quite a shame that Mr Fry, in his wisdom, had discontinued making the mixed cream bar in 1992, it was a top-rated superb product. It consisted of a dark chocolate bar with different cream centres in each section. One with a lime cream filling, one cream raspberry, one cream vanilla, one orange cream and slightly hideously a coffee cream segment. Maybe that was the reason they stopped making them?

(Coffee cream, in my opinion, should be forbidden and banished off the face of the earth. There is no place in this world for any hideous coffee confectionery along with coffee creams and chocolate Revels. Coffee should be for drinking with the primary intention of purely waking you up. Outside that, it has no business as a flavour for sweets. I would ban tiramisu while I am at it. But I digress and feel better for getting that off my chest.)

The old lady slowly pondered at the Jakemans cough sweet selection and coughed very dramatically and ridiculously loud.

"Oh, dear!" said, Fabulous Alice. "That's a nasty cough! I find Jakemans are excellent for helping with coughs. They are the only recipe that is helpful in my experience."

The old lady glared at her as if she was speaking Martian and remained silent. She let out another loud, exaggerated cough. This time she barely covered her mouth. Alarm bells began to ring in Fabulous Alice's ‘difficult-customer-radar’. Generally, in a shop, you can tell within two minutes of meeting a fellow human how hard the sale will be. For instance, Mr Todd likes nothing more than a lengthy chat about the state of the economy before he will hand over money for his Edinburgh rock. Whereas Mrs Parkhouse wants to get home for her favourite antiques programme on the TV, so she hasn't got time to chatter when she picks up her liquorice wheels. On this occasion, she knew it was a hard-labour sale.

She stared at Fabulous Alice for what seemed to be an eternity. Fabulous Alice was quite unsure of how this particular transaction was going to pan out. Still, instinct suggested it was not going to be simple, and she was correct.

"How much is that lollypop behind you?" the old lady spluttered into her white silk hanky and pointed behind Fabulous Alice's shoulder. Fabulous Alice turned to the jar and looked away for a split second.

She turned back. "10p" she informed the old lady.

"I'll take two" she snapped promptly and accompanied her instruction with an extra loud fake cough. As Fabulous Alice turned her back to open the jar and pull out the two red fruit lollipops. The old lady, quick as a flash opened the top of her shopping trolley lid and swiped over twenty odd bars of Fry's peppermint creams clean inside her trolley. Fabulous Alice heard a thud but thought nothing of it.

She had a £20 note ready to hand over to Fabulous Alice and snatched the lollipops and mountain of change. She bolted as fast as she could out the door, down the street and vanished into the camouflage of the Nanna army outside. She could move jolly quickly when she wanted to Fabulous Alice noted. Fabulous Alice returned to the Fry's orange creams to finish her stock display. She rubbed her eyes and couldn't believe that nearly half the box of peppermint creams was empty. Fabulous Alice was sure it was a full fresh box a moment ago because she had not long put them out before the old lady arrived. Hadn't she? There were no other customers in between. So where could they be? She started to doubt the peppermint creams had ever been in there in the first place. Perhaps it wasn't a full box? Maybe she had dropped some? Surely that doddery old lady wasn't quick enough to pull the wool over Fabulous Alice's eyes? She was just a sweet old lady with an innocent cough. Or just maybe the old lady had swiped them? But the latter seemed utterly ridiculous, too ridiculous. Why would an old lady steal from a sweet shop? Fabulous Alice carried on with the rest of her shift as usual and put it down to her own unfortunate judgemental stock error. Perhaps she needed more sleep or a cup of coffee to wake herself up? Fabulous Alice felt a little silly for accusing a sweet old lady of stealing. She popped the kettle on and continued with her eventless day.

A few weeks later, Granny Bubbles was on a shift on her own. The same thing happened all over again. Jakemans. Lollipops. £20 note. Missing peppermint creams. Granny Bubbles had put the doubt down to feeling a little tired and popped the kettle on for a coffee. She thought she must be going mad.

The next week both Fabulous Alice and Granny Bubbles were unloading a large batch of fresh stock into the shop and displaying it all neatly on the shelves. Including all the Fry's selection. Three shiny new boxes of each flavour. Not a single unit had been sold at that moment. The old lady slowly entered sporting a different light blue flowery silk headscarf this week.

Jakemans. Lollipops. £20 note. Then, she reaches in for the peppermint cream heist. Only this time by coincidence Granny Bubbles was standing right behind the old lady. At the same time, Fabulous Alice has turned her back and fetched the two lollipops from the jar.

Granny Bubbles rubbed her eyes in amazement. How bold was this old lady was stealing right in front of her eyes? She was sliding the Peppermint Creams into her trolley of wickedness while belting out a significant fake cough. The Peppermint creams that Granny Bubbles had driven twenty miles and collected herself. Granny Bubbles had parted with hard-earned cash at the wholesalers. Granny Bubbles was as cross as badger and was just about to unleash a venom from the pit of her being. Only, just then the shop bell tingled, and in walked Police Constable Vera McNitty for her weekly Chocolate Peanuts. What luck!

Granny Bubbles ushered her over in a quiet corner to explain the situation. Before the sweet old lady could get to the door, PC McNitty asked to see inside her trolley. Reluctantly and as slowly as she could, the old lady peeled off the trolly lid. She tried to look at the floor, behind her or anywhere PC McNitty was not looking. She knew she was bang in trouble.

They all collectively peered into the trolly at once. To Granny Bubbles amazement, it was half full of her Fry's Peppermint Creams. Months' worth of stock, hundreds of them. All three ladies looked at each other somewhat bewildered. PC McNitty scratching her head.

What on earth was she going to do with over two hundred Fry's Peppermint Cream Bars?

Granny Bubbles didn't know whether to laugh or cry. The thought of someone stealing from her made her cross, but the absurdity of this old lady stockpiling them in her trolley for no apparent reason made her want to laugh. She wasn't even eating them. She always paid for her lollipops with a £20 note, so she HAD the money. It just didn't make any sense.

PC McNitty stared sternly at her waiting for an explanation. When no explanation seemed to be forthcoming, she bent down and homed in on her face and looked carefully under the scarf and recognised her immediately. Her eyes widened in shock and gasped.

"Ma'am? Is that you?"

The old lady blushed and burst out laughing.

Lady Kitty Ellis had been the Chief of Police in the City for as long as PC McNitty could remember. She had busted criminals for a living and nailed some of the top crimes of the century.

There was once a colossal train robbery whereby a bunch of cockney thieves hijacked a train headed for Birmingham. Loaded on board were millions of pounds in old used cash headed for the Royal Mint for burning. It was tattered and ripped to be shredded and mushed into brand new notes.

In the thieves' wisdom, they thought they could intercept the train, make off with all the old notes and live happily ever after in a life of luxury. Unfortunately for them, they discussed their plans in a cafe run by

Lady Kitty Ellis's cleaner's sister, friend's cousin. Loo Brown. Loo let them carry on with their extensive planning and eaves dropped as much as she could, gathering intelligence and forwarding it straight on to her cousins' friends, sister and the cleaner straight on to Lady Kitty directly. It was a wonder anything didn't get mixed up!

Lady Kitty rounded up her best police force and disguised them as regular commuters. They had pictures of the gang so made sure they sat close by each one of them. Like clockwork, the train stopped in Northamptonshire halfway. The train driver Edward had been pre-warned and issued a bullet proof vest under his uniform. He knew all about the heist from police and played along beautifully. While the ultra-polite thieves asked him to sit aside while they hijacked his train, Edward opened his jam sandwiches, lay back and watched events unfold. Which was possibly the most exciting thing to ever happen on his shift or indeed his life. Sometimes a sheep may have wandered onto the track or a few wet leaves, but that was your lot train driving.

Lady Kitty let them unload into a waiting getaway vehicle which turned out to be an ice-cream van. THIS was genuinely their plan. Who would have suspected a bright pink ice cream van as a getaway car? Once the hessian sacks of money were loaded into the ice cream van through the serving hatch. Police watching every move. Lady Kitty had her police spring into action and surround the cash filled ice cream van with armed officers.

"Freeze" Ordered an armed police officer. One of the thieves pulled out a lemon and lime ice lolly and handed it to the officer. "You freeze" She replied laughing. Lady Kitty smirked quietly, and the lady thieves all paused before laughing out loud. They knew they had been caught red handed, but still retained their manners and dignity. It was most odd.

Eventually they politely cuffed all eight middle-aged, well dressed, well-mannered female thieves. Who looked more like they shopped at Waitrose than plan robberies?

But before Lady Kitty sent them to prison for a very long time and just before the ice cream van left for impounding for evidence, the police team all had a 99 ice-cream with a flake and sauce to celebrate. It was hailed a tremendously successful operation, and both Lady Kitty and Loo Brown were awarded police honours and medals.

Lady Kitty was married to Lord Ellis, who liked a quiet country life in his Manor House. She was the polar opposite of him seeking thrills wherever she could. Lady Kitty was so courageous and determined and made it right up to the top of the force. She was legendary. Having foiled thieving attempts on the Queen's personal paintings and her royal jewellery, she had intercepted a million-pound money-printing factory pretending to print T-shirts. The list went on, but when Lady Kitty had retired, she was so bored of doing absolutely nothing, her mind was still too busy to just stop, and she just couldn't switch off her thrill-seeking side.

She had gone from chasing criminals to chasing birds off her beanstalks in the vegetable patch.

The boredom got too much, and she slowly sniffed out some thrills of her own, this time she was a robber. She didn't want or need the Fry's Peppermint Creams. It was just the thrill of not getting caught.

PC McNitty was in the awkward position of sorting out a solution that involved her hero. Lady Kitty was delighted she'd been found out but hadn't given much thought to the consequences. PC McNitty pleaded with Granny Bubbles to agree not to press charges on her favourite work hero and inspiration. She was, after all, the reason PC McNitty went into the force. She made Lady Kitty promise with all her heart not to do it again. She handed back all the stolen goods.

Granny Bubbles knew she could sell the bars again as they were a top seller. She hadn't lost anything as they were all accounted for. With that in mind, they took back all the stock and put it in the store cupboard.

Lady Kitty apologised and invited them to the manor for afternoon tea. Both Granny Bubbles, PC McNitty and Fabulous Alice paid her a visit to listen to Lady Kitty's stories all afternoon. It was great fun.

She didn't get off scot-free though. Granny Bubbles insisted on banning her from ever entering the shop again but, would continue to bring her lollipops once a month to the manor and have a cup of tea with her.

Chapter Seventeen

Pirates and Pineapple Cubes

Mr Wilbur was a pleasant gentleman in his early retirement years. He had frequented Granny Bubbles Sweet Shop for a very long time, as long as it was open in fact. Mr Wilbur would visit each week, mainly to buy his favourite Merry Maid caramels. These were a tasty toffee; they were ellipsoid in shape (squashed sphere) and smothered in delicious creamy milk chocolate. Beautifully wrapped in gold foil with an additional gold cellophane coat for added freshness. These were his childhood favourites. Explaining to Granny Bubbles that he bought them in a white paper bag from his local sweet shop every Saturday. He and his little brother would share a whole bag whilst standing high on a grass mound that peeped down onto his beloved football team called "The Cobblers" (the name for Northampton Town football team). Cobblers were called so because of the town’s magnificent shoemaking industry.

The boys had just about enough for a bag of Merry Maids to share but didn't have enough money for a match ticket each week, so this was the next best thing, and they probably had the best view anyway. During half time they would wrestle and box each other until the whistle started play again. The main aim was not to fall down the hill, and if one of them did, they would have been declared the loser and had to carry the other on his back all the way home. There were only ten months in age between them, so it really was a fair fight. The taste of Merry Maids always brought back happy memories of those days for Mr Wilbur. In adult life, if he was feeling generous, he would buy an extra bag for his now grown-up brother, and they would go and watch the match on a Saturday. They had enough money for season tickets and were too old and creaky for hill wrestling now but would still jostle and fight for the best seat in the stadium.

Granny Bubbles didn't like stocking Merry Maids at all. They were exceedingly popular with pensioners, and the jars ran out very quickly. If word got out and one pensioner knew that they were back in stock, in they would totter, one by one, stock piling as if they were rationed. Granny Bubbles couldn't ever seem to keep up with the insatiable demand. The very sneaky manufacturer had slowly reduced the amount in the wholesale jar until it was half full. But rudely, it still cost the same amount to buy. It was a very sly tactic, and most confectioners were too busy to notice. But because it was a popular selling sweet, Granny Bubbles had no choice but to keep selling them even if she wasn't making any money (which she wasn't). But she continued to stock them in the hope that her customers might buy something else while she had their attention, and they nearly always did with a bit of persuasion. It didn't matter so much with Mr Wilbur though, as Granny Bubbles had been at school with his daughter Hettie, and she was a dear friend.

Hettie was a charming girl at school and seemed to coast through without any drama or negative attention. Just a sweet girl to be around. She worked hard at school and loved learning. She was far too academic to notice any of the other girls' drama or nonsense. Violet Rose was very fond of her for this very reason. She and Hettie would often swap raspberries in her packed lunch in return for Hettie's Pink Lady Apple. Violet Rose had eaten quite enough of the fruit from her own farm to last a lifetime, she was always happy for a swap, and Hettie just adored raspberries. The key was not doing it anywhere near or insight of Jones-Jerms. If Jones-Jerms had gotten wind of the transaction, she would have made such a fuss. Then Hettie, because she was too kind, would feel obliged to hand over the fresh red raspberries and take her cruddy old, battered pear that had been banging around in her lunchbox for days. But Hettie Wilbur was too polite to say no to Jones-Jerms and would more often than not be seen sloshing the mushy pear around her mouth at lunchtimes. She would rather suffer the mushy pear than see Jones-Jerms unhappy. Besides, Hettie had her nose firmly in a history book most of the lunchtime to notice even eating. Which made Granny Bubbles all the more surprised when she found out what she had done for a living.

Along with the weeks Merry Maids, Mr Wilbur had started buying large bags of pineapple chunks and pear drops. He had asked if these could be stored into a sturdy double plastic bag. It had to be able to fit into

Hettie's baggage when she was away. "Where is the lovely Hettie off to Mr Wilbur?" Said Granny Bubbles in her usual chirpy tone.

"She has been deployed to West Africa this time, so we need a triple bag to keep the sweets safe and fresh and probably a little cool" he declared. Dutifully she prepared the sweets just as he required and sealed them tight shut with a few extras for good luck.

After the girls had finished schooling, Hettie's exam results were exceptional. She had thrived at school and relished all the teaching she could suck up. She was like a sponge and could not get enough knowledge inside her brain. She lived for history, specifically British war and was utterly fascinated and learnt all the weapons, artillery, tactics and plans. Her in-depth thirst for all thing's military was a significant factor in choosing her occupation. Desperate to be part of the combat and maybe make history herself one day.

As soon as she was old enough, she enrolled in a military officers' academy for the Royal Navy. Without so much as a look behind her shoulder, Hettie packed up her belongings and skipped off to military school. Mrs Wilbur was frightened to death about her little girl going off to sea to fight. Her mind reeled with a thousand scenarios that could harm Hettie, and her poor mother's belly churned with fear. But Hettie was fearless, and in her head, it was her absolute destiny. Even though there was only one other girl in the school, Hettie barely noticed being surrounded by boys all the time. She saw them as equals, and they did her too.

They knew Hettie was an exceptionally hard worker and respected her for it even more. Just as she did at school, she gave her all to the military academy. She sailed through her exams to become top of the class. Her confidence and strength grew every day. She was exactly where she wanted to be.

Before long she was qualified to the hilt and headed off for missions with The Royal Navy. She was assigned on HMS Queen Edith. It was a colossal destroyer, and the only purpose for existence was to do what it said on the tin: DESTROY. Hettie was more than excited to be on this ship and on this particular mission. That summer, HMS Queen Edith left port in South of England. She headed for the Indian Ocean where her adventures began as a trainee Weapons Engineer.

On the west coast of Africa sat a small quiet country. The country had been developing terrible trouble within its own government, who between them could not agree on how the country should be run. So instead of being harmonious and sensible, they all rather unhelpfully fought with one another for authority and power. In doing so, they lost all control of police, army, navy, firefighters, schools and hospitals. Everything that made a country civilised had sadly fallen apart. It was in a very sorry state and was such a shame that they could not come together to run things effectively. That meant that their own navy that had once protected its own waters were disbanded. The land was no longer able to defend itself, and the fishermen had no protection for their livelihoods. Many of the fishermen had happily made a living and were stable and comfortable up until that point.

It suddenly meant other fishermen from other countries would come to steal the precious fish. Hauling massive amounts of stock that had once been carefully looked after. There was such greed by the alien fishermen that it made the original fishermen furious. Soon, neither fisherman had anything to fish! Large fish had been caught so could no longer breed and small fish were fished too until all of them were gone. As if that was not bad enough ghastly big ships freely dumped their waste of plastic and poo into the fishing areas, sadly killing all the fish.

Knowing that the waters were unprotected brought various problems and put the fishermen in a difficult position. This meant the fishermen had to protect themselves and the area of sea where they needed to fish. So, they clubbed together to form a little fishermen's army. Because they had no formal training in protection, they took it upon themselves to bring weapons on their boats, thus turning them instantly from fishermen into PIRATES.

Because they had no way of making any money through selling fish anymore and they were very cross, they sadly turned to crime. The pirates would board foreign ships and vessels and demand ransoms of money for the release of their captains and ships. Having no choice, companies and countries who needed to pass through the waters paid these ransoms, and it became standard practice. That is until the rest of the world found out, and they were furious at the behaviour of the pirates. Many countries clubbed together to send their navy vessels to help control the area and create some calm.

Hettie was amongst them on her ship. She was learning all about weapons deployment and how to look after the weapons on her new destroyer home. Granny Bubbles was astonished to find out sweet little apple swapping Hettie Wilbur was involved with blasting pirates into oblivion. Only if she needed to mind! That had not happened just yet though. It sounded very farfetched, but it was all 100% true.

The presence and threat of an enormous destroyer that could sizzle the pirates into carbon forever made the pirates back down, and soon they stopped high jacking. The worst pirates were caught and went to jail. HMS Queen Edith targeted and chased off the illegal rubbish dumping ships too, and the waters cleared up in no time. Eventually, the fish even came back, and new fishermen were able to safely make a living and look after the environment.

Until the government had sorted itself out again and come to an agreement on how and who should be in charge, the waters were patrolled for the fisherman by the Royal Navy. Eventually, the country got itself back in order and peace was resumed.

Once Hettie had finished her first deployment, her career went from strength to strength. Her job took her off at sea with many missions intercepting illegal alcohol smugglers in Scotland, patrolling British waters to keep them safe. Peacekeeping in far-flung foreign oceans and sometimes delivering essential aid to countries in need after they had war, devastation or drought. It was a fascinating job. But she did occasionally get a little homesick. It was then that she would head to her locker and pull out a pineapple cube or a pear drop. The pears sometimes reminded her of home and happy school memories. She would pop them in her mouth and savour them slowly until she felt energised enough to keep working hard for her country again. She was amazing. Mr Wilbur was always so keen to show off all of Hettie's adventures. Mrs Wilbur, on the other hand, hated every moment she was away and never stopped worrying about her.

Later Hettie fell in love with a fellow Navy captain. She decided she would put her pirate fighting days aside to raise a family much to Mrs Wilbur's delight. Hettie had two boys who were fellow thrill-seekers like her and gave her a run for her money. She sometimes wondered if it wasn't easier fighting pirates than raising her two boys. Taking them all over the world during school holidays. They would look for adventures and being as close to the sea as possible. She always took pineapple cubes and pear drops with her.

Chapter Sixteen

Imps and Funerals

"Granny Bubbles, do you have any 'Imps'? " Enquired the local vicar in a quiet voice, as he scanned the zillions of glass jars, with his eyes nearly popping out. "I do indeed, Father Patrick! I keep them over here in the winter section" replied Granny Bubbles. It was her personal ambition to ensure during the working day that she was able to say "Yes!" for every customer's request that entered the shop. Her policy was that, if she could not find it, she would seek the recipe and make it herself. She scoured the land for historical recipe books. If she was not in the sweet shop serving or making confections, then Granny Bubbles was knee-deep in recipe books at home in front of the fire. Researching sweets was a part-time job in itself, and she absolutely relished it and sucked up all the knowledge she could find, like a sponge.

Imps, by the way, were tiny black sweets. Think...the size of a pinkie fingernail. They tasted much like they could blow-your-head off, extra-strong with menthol and intense liquorice flavours. These were a hard-core confection and not for the frothy headed population. The sweet-tooth folk would never care much for these mighty bombs of flavour infliction. More like tiny pellets of medicine, and if you were a kid who HAD to have them for a sore throat, you would clasp your lips together, tighter than a bagpipers' knees so as not to ingest them. These pellets of soulless anger were generally for people who had to look after their throats and voices by profession like singers, actors, radio presenters and of course clergymen. Let's put it this way, you wouldn't eat them if you didn't need to.

Father Patrick O'Boyle of St Brendan's Church had to screech the preach of his sermons, at least three times a week. Projecting across the whopping great area of his 14th-century church with as much enthusiasm and vigour as he could muster. It was exhausting. He didn't have any fancy microphones or speakers like some wealthy churches—such an ancient church with draughts blowing all over the place. Usually scorching in the summer and freezing in the winter with nothing in between. This wreaked havoc with his vocal cords. His voice was obviously critical to delivering the message of the good Lord, so he had to look after it well. It often felt like he was going to wear his voice away at the end of each service. Granny Bubbles Sweet Shop proudly played its part in helping his voice stay tiptop.

Father Pat's sermons, at the beginning of his career, were not exactly captivating. He was still quite timid and didn't really project his voice loud enough to command attention. He lost their attention quite a lot, and most of the congregation ended up nattering to each other before the last hymn. Father Pat wondered to himself if his allotted parishioners were sent by God to test him to his limits. Luckily, he liked a challenge.

As time passed, Father Pat noted the routines of people within his church. Most people sat in the same place each week. Most people behaved the same way, and most people had a questionable reason for attending at all. Old Mrs Wince, who was hard of hearing, rather unhelpfully, sat as far away as possible from the pulpit so she could barely hear a word. She would regularly interrupt the service with: "Excuuuuuse meeeeeeeee Faaaaather Pat ...What is the hymn number we are on nowwwwww? " Bellowing far and wide across the church.

Father Pat would look up from his text and sigh. Wondering why the old battle-axe doesn't move closer. He mustered up a smile. " 156 Mrs Wince. ONE. FIVE. SIX." Pointing at the visible hymn number displayed in the service leaflet. Thus, waking up Mr Turnpike, who forever took mass as an opportunity to sneak in a nap while hiding under his peaked cap. Mr Turnpike generally sat napping sweetly near the front, gently snoring which did nothing for Father Pat's ego or confidence.

Worse still, Dr Bone, the local GP attended church on his own each week with bright orange earplugs clearly visible in each ear and with the Sunday Times tucked under his arm. " Morning, Morning, Morning" He nodded to all his patients. Jostling to his regular seat near the front. He made no attempt to hide the enormous newspaper rustling as he turned the pages throughout the session in full view of Father Pat. Father Pat liked to assume the earplugs were to deflect anybody from asking him silly health questions rather than not listen to the lord's words. But it was probably a bit of both.

Mrs Baker thoughtfully chose to knit during the whole session, clashing her knitting needles together during the entire service, making as much noise as possible in the echo of the church. Sniffling and coughing as she went. Father Pat observed her speed and wondered that she may cause sparks to fly off her knitting needle one day and set her nylon cardigan on fire. The congregation were simply either too loud or not listening at all. Week after week, he struggled. He loved his vocation, but they all seemed hell-bent on making his job harder than it needed to be. Eventually, all he really wanted to do was take his service and get back to his real love. His real passion was Hollywood movies! But he was obviously committed to the church, and he had to step it up a gear and try to grab their attention somehow. He would just have to get creative.

Lucy and Melissa were two mischievous young teen sisters who hid behind the tall stone pillars each Sunday. " Morning Faather Pat" they would say in tandem with a grin. Their parents took the opportunity to have a lay in bed in peace each Sunday and sent the girls out. Father Pat noticed the generous contribution of pound notes placed in the collection basket by the girls, so he didn't make a fuss about the unspoken creche. St Brendan’s was in a bit of a state and needed money desperately for patching up an area of broken roof tiles. The rainwater dripped directly onto Father Pat when he stood in the pulpit during lousy weather.

Their incessant giggling regularly disrupted his sermons, passing notes between each other and howling with laughter. " Pahhhhh haaaaaaa haaaa" Melissa would blow out after trying too hard to not laugh out loud. " Shhhhhhhhhhhhhhhhhhhhhhhhh Mellll, we'll get in trouble again!!!" Squeaked Lucy with a chesty laugh and tears in her eyes that she was trying to suppress. Father Pat had to stop again. " GIRLS PLEASE!!!! We need quiet". " SORRY FAAAATHER PAT" They sang in tandem.

One time he discovered why they were so amused. After that Sunday service he found a discarded crumpled note on the floor that read:

The Podgy Priest

"There once was a vicar called Father Pat,

He ate so many sweets, his belly got Fat.

He tried to eat salad to shift a few pounds,

But lost the battle and kept his great mound.

The poor old fat vicar will never be slim,

lucky for us, he can sing a great hymn."

By Lucy Betts,

Bored in church.

This was obviously a source of great hilarity to Melissa, who had burst, mid-prayer, into fits of loud laughter, causing Father Pat to stop and the whole congregation to stare. Now, Father Pat knew why she was so amused.

Poor Father Pat learnt a few hard lessons when he first arrived. He had to think outside the box and work hard to keep his audience engaged and found inventive ways to do so. Maybe now was the time he could sneak in his love for Hollywood within his work? It was worth a try. He started experimenting with his services, assuming that nobody was listening anyway, addressing his sermons as a character other than himself. He found great joy pretending to be someone else. For example, one Tuesday evening mass, he preached the entire sermon in the manner of an American civil war, romantic drama, all in a broad nasal southern American accent. "HalLowed Be thYYY naMe, thYY KingDOM ComE, thYY wiuLL Bee DuN. Ownn EaRth Azz it IZZ iNN HeaVennn."

A good few of the congregation were left a little baffled. Still, the worshippers enjoyed it none the less, Dr Bone even raised his gaze from the stocks and shares page and removed one earplug to listen in. Mrs Baker halted knitting for a moment, losing a stitch.

" AYe MenN!!!!" Finished Father Pat, raising his hand to his brow. Dramatically followed by a self-propelled plummet down the altar steps with Father Pat's priest cape theatrically covering his entire body. He was terrific, award-winning possibly. He rose to applause, thanked everyone and theatrically strutted towards the vestry. He liked the applause, it made him feel great, much better than being ignored. It was the buzz he wanted to feel more often.

There was another curious occasion where Father Pat mimicked a silent mime artist, with white face makeup, black beret and white gloves too.

Throughout the Christening of a new-born baby girl called Esmae Rose. The beautiful baby Esmae was dressed head to foot in white lace. She seemed to enjoy the silence right up until the freezing holy water trickled slowly over her new pink forehead. Father Pat put on a surprised face with a wide-open mouth and covered his white-gloved hand over his mouth. "

"Whaaaaaaaaaaaaaaa!!!!!!!!" Esmae's ear curdling

infant screams echoed throughout St Brendan's, shaking a few loose stained-glass panes out of their lead frames. It was all, quite comical as Christenings went. The Christening party followed along with the mime in the interest of motoring on with the service. Then they could all get to what they thought was the best part—the big party afterwards at the cricket club with fresh buffet food and a free drinks bar.

Parishioners were treated to a sublime version of mass in the manner of 1960's gangsters of New York. "In the Name Owv the fWather, the errrrrr Sunnn and the Howley Spiri, Awwww MeynN." Practising his formidable Italian/American accent with a dusty, slow, menacing tone. To hear the lord's prayer in such aggressive vocals was not only frightening to the small children but bemusing to any newcomers. As word spread about Father Pats unusual sermons though, more people attended. Which was great for Father Pat's hair. The more worshippers left money in the collection tray meant the roof at least was fixed in no time.

While his commitment to the good Lord was never in question, he had finally realised he always had a burning desire inside to be an actor. A kindly churchwarden suggested he might like an acting class she had seen at night school. The Northants Actors Association would dramatically saunter into her classroom after her evening flower arranging class on a Wednesday night at the local college. His eyes brightened like saucers and blushed as he had thought he'd kept his desires under wraps.

It seemed that everyone enjoyed church much more in his character's. Each week was different from the next, and if he had Lucy and Melissa's attention, then it was only a good thing.

Father Pat took part in the village pantomime for a few years. Once he got a little carried away with his character while practising in the church. His role was the Evil Captain Crook in Sinbad for the pantomime. He stopped short of sending a group of choir boys tumbling off a long wooden pew (the plank) whilst he pointed a long candle extinguisher (a sword). "Ahhh haarrrrr, to your death you pesky bandits" He bellowed in a well-rehearsed pirate's voice. The choirmaster stopped them just in time from crashing off the end of the plank to uncertain injury.

Funerals were always an excellent opportunity to practice a bit of method acting. Method acting, he learnt at college, was to immerse yourself in the emotion of a character.

Old Mr Wick had died enjoying his hobby of amateur chemistry experimentation. On his final day of living, he took an unexpected turn for the worst when mixing sodium, water and potassium in his shed at the bottom of the garden. Unfortunately, Mr Wick had misread the portion sizes of the flammable elements.

His notes read:

2 Na + 2 H2O ----> 2 NaOH + H22 K222 + 2 H2O ----> 2 KOH + H2I.

Instead of:

2 Na + 2 H2O ----> 2 NaOH + H22 K2 + 2 H2O ----> 2 KOH + H2I.

Two digits out had decided his fate. But that's science for you. Resulting in the whole shed exploding with an almighty bang taking him with it. Mr Wick's eyes were not as sharp as they had been, you see. He was 98 and had good innings. His loving family agreed he died doing exactly what he loved.

Father Pat honed a well-timed tear for the family just as the coffin was lowered. His eyes flowed with water freely on command. Then, he lost himself for a moment and began to let out cries of grief and collapsed in a dramatic heap over the freshly dug mound, left of the grave. It was such a convincing show of emotion that Mrs Wick came over to comfort him! It was at this point with one eye open on the mound that he realised his acting career could all be a real-life possibility. If he could convince a poor grieving widow, he was home dry? He snapped out of the dramatic emotion pretty sharpish after he, for a moment, forgotten that he still had a job to complete. The funeral and the newly formed widow should have been comforted by him, not vice versa. He continued to practise fake crying at funerals but for the future, stopped just short of the need for comfort.

Father Pat acted in great detail, emotions of joy at christenings and grew more dramatic with his presentations at weddings. Having had a few lessons at the college now, his confidence was through the roof, and he decided it was time to start with real auditioning. It was actually a great success. He immediately got a part in a TV soap about policemen and policewomen on the beat. Father Pat's role was to help criminals find the good Lord while in jail. He excelled in his part as a prison Vicar.

It wasn't long before Father Pat had gotten a little carried away with his alternative career path. He was spending more time at the studio and less time at St Brendan's Church. With his eye off the ball, the result was that he had found himself inside Granny Bubbles Sweet Shop in a blind panic.

Father Pat had forgotten to order the body of Christ for Sunday's service. He was thinking on his feet at 4:45pm on a Saturday afternoon. "I am in a bit of shtick here Granny Bubbles, and I need your help, I've been so busy as an ACTOR on TV" he boomed for all to hear "that I have made a biblical error. I don't suppose you have any rice paper I can buy? I need one hundred portions of holy bread for the body of Christ for Sunday." His voice panicked a little. His usual supplier was 80 miles away, it was Saturday, and the service was on Sunday. There was zero time for anything.

Indeed, Granny Bubbles usually had a supply of rice paper of a sort. However, they had a £50 note printed on them in edible ink. She had sold the last sheet a few hours before, so that option was out. She had another option at hand. Sheets of Tongue Tattoo's which were rice paper circles with little skull and crossbones inked on in food colouring to leave a tiny tattoo on your tongue! But Father Pat had rather hoped not to tattoo his parishioners' tongues, especially with skull and crossbones. If the Arch Deacon found out, he would be in the bad books.

"You're only other option..." said Granny Bubbles pondering and tapping her lips " ...is to use flying saucers??? They are indeed rice paper, but sandwiched with a sherbet filling?" He was not only out of time and running out of options.

"I'll take two hundred flying saucers and all of the tongue tattoos, just in case. It is a solution, and I don't think they will notice anyway" said Father Pat optimistically.

Granny Bubbles weighed out the flying saucers and handed it over the enormous bag. He paid more than his usual £3.50 for 500 holy breads through gritted teeth. Kindly blessed her and the shop and dramatically turned on his heels at what seemed to be one hundred miles an hour with his priest's cape flowing behind him. He hopped into his double-parked vintage car and whizzed away into the sunset back to St Brendan's church. Granny Bubbles chuckled to herself, laughing into a stitch and had to sit down.

It was a little while before she could compose herself again. The congregation would get a surprise this week one way or another with either zingy taste buds or a stained tongue.

That particular week he decided to take the sermon in the manner of Willy Wonker, complete with top hat and cane that he oddly had already in his wardrobe. He themed the service on giving thanks be to God for sugar. Offering prayer to Saint Apollonia, the patron saint of dentistry.

"We thank the lord for sweets and candy.

We thank him very much.

For all the humbugs and the sherbet

and all the Devon creamy fudge.

Dear Lord,

We ask you kindly to find time to bequeath,

The love for Saint Apollonia,

To look after all our teeth.

Amen."

Praised Father Pat. Slapping his bible closed and tottering away in his top hat swinging the cane.

"Amen" Replied the congregation. Those that paid attention found it amusing. Mr Turnpike still didn't bother to rise from his slumber though.

Each worshipper sent into a tizz somewhat when the fizz from the flying saucers made their ears tickle on the way back to the pew.

The choir boys were delighted to scoop up the remains of the bag after service. The organist took a pocket full up with him and played the best Autumn Days hymn he ever had! All in all, it was one of Father Pats best services.

His career never quite reached Hollywood, but he did pursue small acting parts in other soaps and detective programmes but nearly always playing a Vicar! Granny Bubbles managed to find plain sheets of rice paper for the next time Father Patrick was in a mess. But that didn't happen for a while. Worshippers still talked about that service regularly. The church roof was eventually fixed, and a sound system was purchased with the extra money. Granny Bubbles Sweet shop gained a whole new customer base of flying saucers and tongue tattoos.

Chapter Seventeen

Twigs and Spogs

Sometimes, especially during the winter months. Granny Bubbles felt more like a pharmacy than a sweet shop. Phil's Pills the Pharmacy along the High Street sent a daily stream of new customers along most days. This helped pay the landlord's rent, so it was actually an added bonus. When she opened the sweet shop, it had never occurred to Granny Bubbles that she would ever be helping anyone medically.

The demand was high for a helping hand with many a human ailment, and on the upside, Granny Bubbles felt it was quite a good feeling to help people.

There were plenty of conditions to aid. The most common were poop problems, (keeping it in and letting it out), sore throats, chesty coughs, taste loss, weight loss, weight gain, clearing snot from noses and many more. Each day something new would pop up. Granny Bubbles had a solution for most of it. But the biggest medical reason to come into a sweet shop was to cheer up your soul. A bag of Devon Cream fudge could work wonders with that.

Old Jock McFlowers was a retired digger driver and spent many a day tending to his leeks at his allotment. Mrs McFlowers was a grumpy ancient dragon, so he tried to keep out of her way as much as possible. According to Mrs McFlowers, his leeks ought to be fit for the National Vegetable Show with the amount of time he spent tending to them. As he put his wellies on, her bombardment began.

She began to growl at him." If you invested half the time on your marriage as you do them blasted leeks, you might just get somewhere... Jock McFlowers! do you hear me?" It made her cross knowing he was off to the allotment and leaving her with all the work to do. She didn't have anything better to do herself. Still, she loved to make it known he was shirking his responsibility.

"Have you taken the bins out yet? The bin men are coming tomorrow, and I'm not doing it myself?" She grumbled as she pulled the bins around to get on and do it herself.

"Did you clear up that dog poo in the garden? Like I asked you twenty times last week?" Her pitch increasing whilst scouring at the poo on the lawn, picking up the poo bags to do it herself. "NO... I thought not, you're a lazy old clod, you'll be the death of me." She screeched, bending over to clean up each poo.

"For the love of God, you old crow, stop bellowing and come up for air." He thought quietly to himself. Not quite brave enough to reply out loud. Instead, he opted for a chirpier reply "Yes, my darling! See you later".

The further he was, the louder she became, and the faster he picked up speed on foot. He could still hear her barking from afar. "Make sure you are back in time for tea Jock McFlowers, or I'll throw your dinner in the garden for the birds. You see if I don't Jock McFlowers and whilst I am at it you lay off that whiskey you old goat, I know what you are up to!" She shouted louder as he disappeared behind the bushes heading to his happy hut. He moved further away, and he could still hear her words as she continued to bleat with or without his ear. Getting quieter the further away he walked until it was just a muffled din.

Leeks are very slow-growing and can be planted and harvested all year round. This was the perfect crop to get Mr McFlowers out of the house and doing what he did best. He was never happier than hauling around the mud in all weathers with shovels of this, a fork of that and a spade of the other. Knee deep in boggy brown earth was his happy place. No Mrs McFlowers to bother him.

But there was another reason Mr McFlowers was attracted to his allotment. He had set up his own Whiskey making area inside his rickety old shed where he and his fellow allotment cronies called his hut "The Happy Hut". They could all be found chatting in deck chairs, to his fellow gardeners under the pretence of growing things, but each with a jam jar of whiskey in hand. It was all fun and games until it was home time. If Mrs McFlowers could smell one whiff of his whiskey, she would bend his ear until bedtime.

The surprising solution to avoiding Mrs McFlowers wroth was a quick swing by Granny Bubbles Sweet Shop for a bag of Oddfellows on the way home.

These are chalky sweets and were excellent at hiding lousy breath, particularly the pong of whiskey. They were an unusual recipe of floral, spices and fruits. Made only by a phenomenally talented maker in Edinburg called Ross's. If he could hold off on a little drunk wobble, she would not suspect a thing, and she certainly wouldn't smell it. As soon as he was close to getting low, he would be in for more. Soon followed a few more gardeners whom Mr McFlowers must have shared his secret wife weapon.

"A quarter of Marriage Savers please Granny Bubbles," said the Gardeners. "Certainly Sir" replied Granny Bubbles. It always made her smile knowing what they were up to.

The ultra-fussy liquorice customers that would give Granny Bubbles quite a tough time. They were a breed of their own. Often with no regard for other folk waiting in the queue to pick out ONLY their favourites. One man used to come in and demand only the brown, black and white squares from the Liquorice All-Sorts, which worked out well with the lady who asked her to pick out the brown, black and white ones. This, luckily, saved on waste.

Cath, the local Midwife, would regularly pay a visit to Granny Bubbles on behalf of her new mothers, who were, unfortunately, having trouble pooping after birth. The Mums would be treated to a bag of black Liquorice wheels to get things moving, and if that didn't work, it was the ancient solution of a Liquorice Root

Stick. New mothers must have thought she was crazy in the head. Sauntering in with a handful of brown twigs. Advising them, they were a liquorice flavoured twig and instructing them to suck on the twigs to relive their poop issue. But it worked every time. The new mothers were comfortable again afterwards and grateful for the strange but useful advice. The sticks if you haven't ever seen them are the root from the Liquorice bush. They are harvested and made into small bundles and dried out. Then you pick one out and suck the Liquorice flavour out. It's an all-natural solution, people used to do this long before sweets were available. The Liquorice flavour you taste all stems from extracting the flavour from these roots. It is somewhat less offensive than it sounds and is quite delicious, providing you don't splinter your gums on the way!

In the Liquorice section sat an alien confection. 'Spogs.' Technically, these beauties were jelly with an aniseed flavour. But Granny Bubbles had to sit them in the Liquorice section because that's where people expected to find them even though they were not liquorice. They were a tricky confectionery that had their own set of rules. People expected them to be in the Liquorice section because you would generally find them in Liquorice All-sorts. Suppose you cannot imagine what Spogs are. In that case, these are the pink and blue cylindrical jellies with an intense aniseed flavour that you probably hadn't realised were aniseed because you could mistake them for liquorice. Then, they are smothered in tiny spheres of pink or blue sugar balls. They have several different names depending on geographical location. People would ask for the same sweet but with a completely different name.

Mr Savoury would ask for "Spogs" because he was from in the Midlands, Mrs Raymond would require "Horsecakes" because she was from the North of England and Mrs Berryman would say "Jelly Buttons" because she was from Cornwall in the south of England.

Liquorice Allsorts came about, in 1889 a Bassets sales representative visiting a shop managed to drop all of his sweetie samples all over the counter of a potential sweet shop owner customer by mistake. He scooped them all up together in a jar. The confectioner was so impressed with how pretty they looked in the jar that he placed an order there and then. That was how they came to be Liquorice Allsorts.

Liquorice was excellent for assisting a person to go for a poop. It has a laxative effect which helped poop travel quickly through the digestive system and out the other side smoothly.

There are several types of Liquorice consumers. Some just simply cherished the moreish taste and could take a weekly treat and leave it at that. These were called 'sensible people.' Some were far more sinister and thoroughly addicted to the black stuff. They tended to stockpile their favourites. You will see a different side to them if you were low or had no stock. Then there was a spiteful Liquorice breed that only bought liquorice so they didn't have to share it with other Liquorice haters that might be in their house. This could also apply to Floral Gums and Cherry Lips customers. These were similar to a soapy flavour. They were not for sharing either.

Then there were the poor souls diagnosed with a disease called Diabetes. In a nutshell, their bodies had stopped knowing what to do with its own sugar levels. Too much sugar or too little sugar could make them feel very poorly indeed. With Diabetes, it generally meant that sweets were out of bounds. Not wanting to miss out on the great taste of their favourite childhood sweets, these customers could still buy sweets, but they had to be Sugar-FREE. The sugar is replaced with another type of sugar called Isomalt. Isomalt is a sugar alternative. It looked just like regular sugar when boiled, but it was much kinder to their blood sugar levels, so they did not feel poorly. It didn't make the sugar levels change in their bodies. It was hard-boiled and was near impossible to burn so Granny Bubbles loved working with it. When it had colours, and flavours added you couldn't tell the difference. They looked JUST like a hard-boiled sweet and tasted like one too. They were a bit kinder to teeth also. So, sugar-free was a solution to a little treat for people with Diabetes now and again. I say now and again because they are not ideal for troughing down at 100 miles an hour. But there are side effects. One day a lovely group of mums were on a coach trip back from Sunny Hunstanton seaside. Between them, they once accidentally ate a massive bag of sugar-free Rhubarb and Custards on the bus. Twenty minutes later, after the first Mum let out a gigantic windy fart. She blushed, was utterly mortified and apologised in horror with big red, rosy cheeks. Then, so did the Mum next to her. Two more Mums on the opposite isle had to beg the driver to use the loo while the other two were bent over in agony with a rumbling tummy and very loud pumps.

For a short while they thought they were all at death's door until the Mum who had dished out the big bag of sweets realised what had happened! She gasped in horror, looking at the bag

"THEY WERE SUGAR-FREE SWEETS!!!" She yelled. "I'm so sorry!" She recognised the symptoms immediately as this was not the first time, she had whomped down a full sugar-free bag and a similar thing had happened. The last time she dieted, she thought they might assist, in a bid to lose a few Christmas pounds! Luckily her fellow mums saw the funny side and laughed, and every time another one of them farted they laughed even more. They were grateful knowing they would not die and drank plenty of water to wash it all through.

During the winter months was all about cough sweets. Grays Herbal Candy made from, and an unusual herb called Horehound (that John the pony enjoyed). These were great for coughs and sore throats. Army and Navy, Fisherman's Friend, Pink and White Clove Drops. Cough Candy too which was also made from clove oil and was not to be mistaken with Aniseed Twists which are made with aniseed! These were all great for coughs.

To clear a blocked nose was a eucalyptus sweet called Jakemans. Another top seller was old-fashioned Winter Mix consisted of Mints, Aniseed, Cough Candy, Liquorice and Clove. Everything you'd need to keep sniffles away!

One tiny old lady used to visit to buy giant Marshmallows. She said she ate one before bed and then again at 2 am when she awoke. She swore blind they helped her settle. Any excuse for a marshmallow in bed is good, in my opinion.

Granny Bubbles loved the thought that her sweets helped people when they felt poorly. She was a bit mortified at the Mums feeling ill on the bus when she gave them to her friends by mistake. She really ought to have known better. She was also one of the farter's, so she didn't get away with it either. At least they could now look back and laugh.

Chapter Eighteen

Sherbet and Frogs

There were times when Granny Bubbles had wished she hadn't entered the world of confectionery at all. It was hard, heavy work, and quite often you could not produce sweets because it was too wet, too hot, too cold, too humid or too dry. Granny Bubbles had made all the mistakes in the book. But you have to keep ploughing on. Learning from mistakes is how we all grow. That's why you should never be hard on yourself if you make a mistake. Learn from it and do better next time.

Certain types of confectionery had to be made only in prime conditions. It was no good making fudge on a rainy day because the air was too moist to set the fudge without ugly crystals appearing.

Chocolate is a diva of a substance. Chocolate will not perform if it is too hot or too humid or too damp. Have you ever opened a chocolate wrapper seen a chocolate bar with white misty blobs on the chocolate surface? It is, in fact, not mould at all. It is called 'Bloom'. The coco will separate from the cocoa fat, and a fat dusty mist will sit on the top of the chocolate bar. Sometimes this can happen if you leave it in a hot car. When you remember the next day after it has cooled down again, you will find a fat bloom on the top. It's perfectly ok to eat. It's just that you can see the fat now as opposed to it usually sneaking amongst delicious cocoa! If you ever want to see how much fat is in something pop it in boiling water and leave it there for a week. You'll see the fat separate. It's quite surprising!

Granny Bubbles Sweet Shop being in the middle of England. In probably one of the most weather changeable regions in the country. Making sweets was a tricky task indeed. It took Granny Bubbles years of mistakes to gain knowledge of what to make when. But eventually, she had honed a near-perfect system. Before long she was making as much as she could and selling it just as fast.

Not everything had to be cooked. Sherbet uses no heat at all. It is merely ground sugar with added flavour and colour and another ingredient called Citric

Acid. Putting ACID into food sounds terribly dramatic, but it is only an organic acid found in lemons, limes and strangely, fermented mushrooms! It is what gives your tongue a laugh and your ears a tickle when you eat Sherbet Lemons or a Flying Saucer. If you want a fizzy sherbet, then a touch of bicarbonate soda adds a fizz. It fizzes up your nose! In Granny Bubbles Sweet Shop, she had the most extensive range of sherbet in the country.

Rhubarb and custard flavour was always on-trend. The sparkly pink sherbet tasted of tangy rhubarb and the yellow flavoured of creamy custard. There was even a Gin and Tonic flavour. Her absolute favourite to make was Rainbow Sherbet. Rainbow sherbet was many different layers of colour and flavour. It had blue raspberry, pink cherry, yellow lemon, green mango, orange... well orange was orange! Purple was a delicious plumb flavour too. She also started making batches for other sweet shops and was soon busier than an Elf at Christmas. The whole shelf rammed with forty different concoctions of sherbet. You'd be surprised what people used them for too. One lady bought them to dye her wool yarns. A local barman bought it for dipping the top of his glass rims ready for fancy cocktails, and bakers used them for cupcake toppings, but the biggest consumer were Mums buying them on the way home from school.

Mrs Nelly had 8-year-old twin boys who bickered and fought all the way home every day. She soon learned that if they were pre-occupied with dipping their tiny lollipop into a different flavoured sherbet each day, that she could have a long peaceful walk home from school. Before her discovery of sherbet dipping, Mrs Nelly had to contend with fighting, squabbling, lunchbox ninja, book bag whacking and coat hood pulling. It was all she could do to keep her Nelly boys away from the road. Neither of the boys had an ounce of self-awareness between them. She saved their lives on more than one occasion. The sherbet was in relatively small bags, so the boys had to dig deep, concentrate and get the most out of each bag. By the time they reached home, it was time to start squabbling, wrestling and scrapping again. But at least they were away from cars, traffic and people.

The shop window had three giant cocktail glasses and an oversized glass sweet jar for the window display. Granny Bubbles would layer different coloured sherbet to make a pretty window display. She would often find finger holes dipped in the sherbet. People had tried to steal a sneaky finger full of sherbet. It must have tasted quite unpleasant, as it was salt, it had served the thieves right for trying to steal.

She had learnt much from a recipe book that dated back to Victorian times used by all good confectioners. It was called 'Skuse's Complete Confectionery'. It was a fantastic book that was written when Queen Victoria was ruling all she ruled. Allegedly Queen Victoria was most partial to Scottish Tablet and

Sugared Almonds. The recipes and ingredients all stood steadfast and do even today. Nothing had changed at all.

Even with the help of the book, so much more could go wrong. Sugar is weird stuff to work with, and it took practice, skill, patience and money. She destroyed a few hundred kilos of sugar during training. Oh, not to mention the additional weight gain after eating much of it! That is what is called "An occupational hazard".

It took Granny Bubbles over a year of practice before she could confidently even make a boiled sweet. Without too much flavour, too little flavour, too much colour, too little colouring, too much citric acid or too low. Sugar was tricky, sticky, demanding, stuff to work with, and chocolate was equally obnoxious. They are the divas of ingredients.

Granny Bubbles had come a long way since the opening day. She had learnt so much about people, confectionery, staff, accounting and business. There were many, many mistakes made. Each mistake was a lesson that helped her learn and grow. Those that doubted her, their objections propelled her along to prove that she could, would and did make a success of her business. From then on, if people said that she couldn't do something, she knew she was on the right tracks to success. Her handmade confections were extremely popular. Fabulous Alice had been happy to run the sweet shop with help from Maia Moo so that Granny Bubbles could concentrate on making stock.

Her repertoire of sweets soon began to add up. On fresh fudge days, she could sell a whopping 10 kg of fudge in a day. Folk knew when she was making goodie because the smell would waft all the way up the high street. They would come before or after lunch for big batches to take away. It was a top seller. Many stockpiling for the month, just in case they ran short. It was super popular. Word had gotten down to London about her fabulous fudge and a fancy store in Kensington had asked her to make batches to sell in their very posh confectionery department. It was a huge compliment and a great piece of business that would help the company grow.

Instead of buying stock in from the wholesalers, she eventually made nearly everything for the shop herself, which meant much more profits. Fellow confectioners soon began to place orders for their shops too, the business grew and grew.

Such was the demand that Granny Bubbles finally had to travel further afield to seek fresh new flavours and ingredients. This would be an adventure that would take her all around the world seeking fresh ingredients from far flung countries like Sri Lanka, Madagascar and Europe. Granny Bubbles was so pleased she took the risk to start her shop and had ignored all the naysayers. The regulars kept coming and soon she needed a warehouse just like Mr Deans to produce and sell all of her freshly made fudges, Belgian chocolates, sherbets and coconut ices.

It was soon time for me to leave Mr Plums Grocers after I had little time to commit to polishing granny smiths and trimming his bushy onions and if I didn't have to listen the old curmudgeon ever again it would be too soon. I would miss the cruel banter of the Frostette triplets, John the Pony's fluffy main and friendly greetings. Even Godzilla the Monitor lizard. Not to mention all of the captivating customers who used the High Street. But as you know, nothing lasts forever, and I eventually passed my English degree with honours and began writing professionally about a fascinating sweet shop called Granny Bubbles Sweet Shop and all who entered it. What a joy it was to write about her, and her Gobstopping Gossip and she even shared some of her secret recipes so that you can try and make some treats of your own.

Recipe for Mint Choccy Frogs

- Frog mould
- Any Chocolate
- Peppermint OIL

Chop up your chocolate into small pieces

Place in a dry bowl

Pop in the microwave for thirty seconds, stir repeat in ten second bursts until it is all melted

Do NOT be tempted to leave it in the microwave on high for longer as it will burn VERY quickly

OR

Put the bowl in a shallow pan of hot water

and stir until melted

DO NOT get water in the chocolate or you

will ruin it

When melted, add the peppermint oil to taste

You can use lemon or orange oil too but never water-based flavours as they will ruin the chocolate.

When it is ready, pour into frog moulds and leave to set overnight

If you have melted the chocolate slowly and correctly, the frogs will have shrunk and will just pop out with ease because chocolate shrinks as it sets

EAT them before anyone else gets a chance

Recipe for Fizzy Sherbet

Five Hundred grams of Granulated Sugar

One Hundred grams of Citric Acid

- Fifty grams of Bicarbonate Soda
- Any Food Colouring you like
- Any Flavour you want.

Take a quarter of the Granulated Sugar and

place it in a blender or food processor

Add the flavouring and colouring

Add the Citric Acid and the Bicarbonate Soda

Grind altogether into a fine powder

Add the rest of the Granulated sugar to the food processor and grind until the sugar is a fine powder

Keep in an airtight jar

Find your favourite lolly and dip it in as and when you like

Answer: A Chocolate Baaaaa!

Joke from introduction you probably did not read?

Printed in Great Britain
by Amazon

84818116R00231